PUT 'EM UP

Fargo waited until the man was back sitting beside his friend before he stepped into the clearing, his Colt pointed at the two.

Both of them jumped and started to reach for their guns, but Fargo said, "Too early and too cold to die."

Both men froze, half up, half reaching for their guns.

"Sit back down now real slow and put your hands where I can see them."

Both men did as they were told. Now the trick would be getting information out of them. . . .

THE TRAILSMAN

#324

CALIFORNIA CRACKDOWN

by

Jon Sharpe

A SIGNET BOOK

SIGNET
Published by New American Library, a division of
Penguin Group (USA) Inc., 375 Hudson Street,
New York, New York 10014, USA
Penguin Group (Canada), 90 Eglinton Avenue East, Suite 700, Toronto,
Ontario M4P 2Y3, Canada (a division of Pearson Penguin Canada Inc.)
Penguin Books Ltd., 80 Strand, London WC2R 0RL, England
Penguin Ireland, 25 St. Stephen's Green, Dublin 2,
Ireland (a division of Penguin Books Ltd.)
Penguin Group (Australia), 250 Camberwell Road, Camberwell, Victoria 3124,
Australia (a division of Pearson Australia Group Pty. Ltd.)
Penguin Books India Pvt. Ltd., 11 Community Centre, Panchsheel Park,
New Delhi - 110 017, India
Penguin Group (NZ), 67 Apollo Drive, Rosedale, North Shore 0632,
New Zealand (a division of Pearson New Zealand Ltd.)
Penguin Books (South Africa) (Pty.) Ltd., 24 Sturdee Avenue,
Rosebank, Johannesburg 2196, South Africa

Penguin Books Ltd., Registered Offices:
80 Strand, London WC2R 0RL, England

First published by Signet, an imprint of New American Library,
a division of Penguin Group (USA) Inc.

First Printing, October 2008
10 9 8 7 6 5 4 3 2 1

The first chapter of this book previously appeared in *Wyoming Death Trap*,
the three hundred twenty-third volume in this series.

Copyright © Penguin Group (USA) Inc., 2008
All rights reserved

 REGISTERED TRADEMARK—MARCA REGISTRADA

Printed in the United States of America

PUBLISHER'S NOTE
This is a work of fiction. Names, characters, places, and incidents either are
the product of the author's imagination or are used fictitiously, and any resem-
blance to actual persons, living or dead, events, or locales is entirely
coincidental.

The publisher does not have any control over and does not assume any
responsibility for author or third-party Web sites or their content.

The Trailsman

Beginnings . . . they bend the tree and they mark the man. Skye Fargo was born when he was eighteen. Terror was his midwife, vengeance his first cry. Killing spawned Skye Fargo, ruthless, cold-blooded murder. Out of the acrid smoke of gunpowder still hanging in the air, he rose, cried out a promise never forgotten.

The Trailsman they began to call him all across the West: searcher, scout, hunter, the man who could see where others only looked, his skills for hire but not his soul, the man who lived each day to the fullest, yet trailed each tomorrow. Skye Fargo, the Trailsman, the seeker who could take the wildness of a land and the wanting of a woman and make them his own.

California, 1861—the death of a good friend at the hands of ruthless killers means that many will die before the Trailsman feels that his need for vengeance has been satisfied.

1

Skye Fargo eased silently from behind the tree and studied the two men crouched in the bushes ten paces from him. Both had Colts filling their hands.

Their intent was clearly the gold wagon coming down the trail toward Sacramento. And Fargo's business was to protect it.

Fargo knew there were three more gold rustlers on the other side of the wagon road that was the supply line up to Placerville and the mines in the area. It was also the only way to get the gold down to the banks and train lines in Sacramento. . . .

Cain Parker, owner of Sharon's Dream, one of the bigger mines in the area, had begged Fargo to come help him protect his gold between the mine and Sacramento. Cain really didn't need to beg, since he and Fargo had known each other for years and had been back-to-back in their share of fights together. Fargo figured he owed Cain his life a few times over, so anything Cain asked, Fargo would do.

The name of the mine, Sharon's Dream, had come from Cain's late wife, one of the nicer women Fargo had ever met. She had always talked about she and Cain going farther west to search for gold, but it wasn't until after she died that Cain took his son, Daniel, then a teenager, and did just that.

Fargo had arrived at the Sharon's Dream gold mine a little after eight in the morning. The main house was a two-story wood building that looked like it would fit better just outside Boston. It was freshly painted white and stood out in the warm, morning sun against the browns and grays of the dirt and rocks around it. Three long and low unpainted buildings near the edge of the hill looked like bunkhouses, one much larger than the others. The mine opening itself was about halfway up a rock-strewn hillside above and to the right of the bunkhouses, with the mine tailings spreading out below it like a woman's fan.

Placerville had started and gotten its name from an intense gold rush of Placer mining in the streams in the area. But as with most Placers, the gold had to come from somewhere, and soon the miners were digging into the hills, following the veins, or just digging in hopes to find a vein.

From what Fargo understood, Cain had managed to stake a claim to a really rich and long vein that so far showed no signs of playing out. He said it was taking almost thirty men to work the mine in shifts, cooks to keep them fed, and a number of hired guns to guard the place.

As Fargo rode up, Cain came running out of the house.

"Fargo, you old trail hand," Cain said, a huge smile on his face. "You are a sight for sore eyes."

"Didn't know you were having eye problems as well," Fargo said, climbing down from his big Ovaro and shaking his old friend's firm, solid hand. He had to admit, he had missed being around Cain. The two of them just seemed to fit together. Fargo knew a lot of people around the West, but he had very few close friends like Cain.

Cain stood about a fist shorter than Fargo, and was a good ten years older. But the age was only showing on his thinning hairline and the sun wrinkles on his face that disappeared completely when he smiled. The rest of him still looked as solid as a rock.

Cain could smile and laugh with the best of them. And he had the ability to inspire loyalty from those around him. Standing there with his old friend again brought back so many good memories of so many good times.

"How long has it been?" Cain asked, finally letting go of Fargo's hand.

"Too long. Four years, maybe five."

Cain laughed. "Yup, too long. How about we don't let that happen again?" He swung his arm wide, gesturing toward the spread around them. "So, what do you think of Sharon's Dream?"

"Big and impressive," Fargo said, telling the truth. "Sharon would have been proud."

Cain smiled at the memory of his wife. "Yeah, she would have been, wouldn't she?"

"No doubt."

Cain pointed up at the hill above the huge pile of tailings. "It's still pouring out the high-quality ore. In fact, we have a shipment headed to Sacramento today." He pointed to a wagon being loaded.

"Guess my timing is perfect," Fargo said.

"As always," Cain said. "You up for going to work?"

"No better time than the present," Fargo said.

Cain laughed. "I don't know. Some of my memories tell me the past was a pretty good time as well."

Cain introduced Fargo as the Trailsman to his six men that were to guard the shipment, and made it clear that Fargo was in charge of getting the ore to the refinery, even though Cain himself was riding along. Not a one of them seemed to mind. In fact, most of them had heard of Fargo and looked downright relieved he was on the job.

He just hoped he could live up to whatever they had heard about him.

Fargo could tell that four of the men were hired trail hands and were comfortable with their guns. One carried Colts on both hips, and all of them had carbines in sheaths on their horses. The other two didn't look so trail experienced. One, Cain introduced as Hank, his mine foreman. The other was Walt, a young

3

kid with strong-looking arms, a ready smile, and an eagerness to do anything to help.

Fargo had two of the experienced trail hands ride ahead of the wagon with carbines across their saddles, two behind, and Walt and Hank on the wagon. Cain was driving the wagon and Hank sat beside him. Walt sat on the gold boxes, riding backward to make sure no one came up behind them.

Cain said he had lost three good men so far in the last six shipments, but had managed to get the gold out every time. But the robbers had gained in numbers each time, and it seemed like the focus was on Cain's shipments more than the other mines in the area.

Fargo didn't much like the sound of that. Sure, Cain was doing well, but if he really was being targeted, that meant there was a lot more behind this than just a gang of robbers taking opportunities as they came down the trail.

As they pulled onto the main Placerville road from the Sharon's Dream side road, Fargo had the wagon slow down. He wanted to give himself time to scout ahead on his big Ovaro stallion.

As the wagon moved slowly along, he was often a good distance from the road, moving along high ground to scout out what was ahead before circling back. He knew the Placerville road. He had been in the area a number of times as the gold boom exploded. With luck, he could clear this band of robbers out of the area in a few weeks, while enjoying some time with his old friend.

It was from a ridgeline to the north of the trail that he saw the five men taking up positions in a stand of tall trees and thick brush to ambush the gold shipment.

He had left his horse and moved silently down on them.

From the looks of the two men crouched in front of him, Cain had gotten Fargo on the job just in time. The wagon and the men guarding it didn't stand a chance against five guns blazing a short distance from the narrow corridor between the trees.

The two thieves were dressed like miners. They wore stained and faded overalls over dirty white undershirts, rough work boots, and thin-brimmed hats. These men were not professional robbers. They had been hired by someone to do this, which meant Cain had a much bigger problem than these five. This was no gang of trail thieves and gun sharps. This sounded like another mine owner with money who was after the gold ore coming out of Sharon's Dream.

The rumbling of the heavy wagon echoed ahead through the trees and brush, and the two men both raised their guns, their attention completely on the road. With his Colt in hand, Fargo stepped toward them.

Fargo could move silently like a mountain lion when he wanted to. He was within a step of the closest robber when the man glanced around and said, "What . . . ?"

It was his last word before Fargo smashed his fist into the man's face, the punch slamming him back into a boulder. The man slid down, unconscious.

"No!" Fargo said, pointing his Colt at the other man, who was just now turning to fire on Fargo.

Fargo put two bullets into the man's right shoulder. Fargo could see him teeter, then fall to the ground. But the man wasn't done yet. Lying flat on his back, he fired as he brought his gun up, his shot smashing wide and splattering into a tree behind Fargo. Fargo put two quick shots into the miner, then ducked behind a tree to make sure he was out of the way of fire coming from across the trail.

"Harry!" someone shouted from across the road. This one was hiding in a stand of trees about thirty paces away and slightly up the road toward the wagon.

It seemed that one of the two men had been named Harry. Fargo didn't much care which one. They had planned on bushwhacking and killing good men trying to do an honest day's work. They didn't even deserve names on the crosses over their graves. Actually, as far as Fargo was concerned, they were better served as buzzard meat.

One man eased out from behind a tree, glancing first up the road at the now stopped wagon and then over at where his friends were.

"Get back!" another robber said from his hiding place.

At least one of them had a slight bit of sense.

Taking no chances, Fargo aimed at the man who had left his cover and smashed his gun hand with a clean, quick shot. The man spun like he'd been dancing with a pretty girl in a saloon, then went over backward in a dance move no one would ever want to try to repeat.

Two guns opened up, splintering bark chest-high from the tree Fargo was using as a shield.

Fargo dropped to the ground, spotted where one gun was firing from, and patterned the area with three quick shots.

The shout of pain and then the sound of a body falling into the brush were clear as Fargo sat with his back against the tree and quickly reloaded all six cylinders.

For a moment, the forest was silent; then came the sound of a man crashing through the brush as the last ambusher ran for his life, trying to make it to where they had tied off their horses.

Fargo dashed across the road, his heavy boots pounding the dust.

Down the road he could see that Cain and his men had done exactly as he had told them to do when they heard gunfire. Cain had pulled the wagon off the road and into the closest shelter available. Everyone had dismounted and taken cover, their guns up and ready.

Up ahead of him, the ambusher was making a lot of noise as he scrambled up the open rock slope to the horses. Fargo burst out of the trees on the other side of the small grove just as the man worked to mount a reluctant steed. He also looked like a miner, but the horse and gear he rode didn't fit him.

And he clearly wasn't used to mounting and riding fast as he struggled to hold the horse still enough for him to get in the saddle.

Fargo took a deep breath. No point in killing him. Fargo almost smiled. The way the man was riding—looking like he was ready to fall off his horse—maybe he'd kill himself anyway.

Carrying his Colt in a ready position, Fargo climbed up the hill the rest of the way to check on the remaining horses. They were well kept and the tack was expensive, the type you'd find the owner of a ranch using, not a fellow dressed like he was fresh out of a mine. Or, for that matter, the man down in the trees who looked like a typical rustler. Someone with money was behind this and had given them good horses for the job.

Marshal Tal Davis pushed his way through the bat-wings and strode into the saloon. He recognized just about everybody in the place.

He was looking for faces he *didn't* recognize. The burly, red-haired man behind the bar who went by the name of Irish was pouring a couple of miners rye when he glanced up and exchanged a familiar look with the lawman. Like all the bartenders in town, Irish was on notice to report any stranger who might be a hired gun. While paid killers didn't all look the same—nor were they the same in age or nationality—they tended to be cocky about their calling. Davis always laughed about how many hired guns got themselves killed in saloon shoot-outs by some local. It wasn't that the locals were so fast on the draw; it was simply that hired guns tended to have mouths as big as their reputations. They often got drunk and got into arguments that left them dead at the hands of a talented—and more sober—amateur.

Irish had sent a runner to tell the marshal that a suspicious-looking man was sitting in the back of the place playing poker and bullying the other four men sitting in.

A long bar of crude pine ran along the west wall. A small stage ran the length of the back wall. The tables filled up the eastern part of the place. A low fog of tobacco smoke hovered over everything.

Davis didn't have any trouble figuring out who the probable gunny was. At the moment the man was slamming his wide fist down against the table, making it dance, toppling poker chips. His harsh voice was made even harsher by his drunkenness and anger. "You think I don't know when a bunch of rubes are cheatin' me?" he said.

The other players watched in shock and fear as the gunny suddenly produced a shiny Colt .45 and pointed it at the face of a bald man.

"You been cheatin' me all along," the gunny said, "and now you're gonna pay."

"This is an honest game, Kelly," the bald man said. He managed to sound calm. "You're havin' a run of bad luck is all. And to be honest, it don't help that you managed to put away all them drinks while we've been playin'. Now my advice to you—"

"I don't want no advice from you!"

The few drinkers who hadn't been watching the card game now swung their attention to the man holding the gun on the cardplayers. They also paid attention to Davis. He now stood no more than six feet in back of the gunny, his own Colt drawn.

"I don't want trouble, mister. I'm the marshal here and as anybody'll tell you, I don't enjoy shootin' people. Now I just want you to turn around slow and easy and hand me your gun without me having to kill you to get it."

The gunny's shoulders and head jerked at Davis's words. His broad back, covered in an expensive white shirt—getting a better grade of gunnies in town, the lawman noted wryly—hunched some and his elbow rose. He was getting ready to turn on Davis and fire.

But the marshal, despite rheumatism, arthritis, and

advancing age, moved with surprising speed. In four quick steps he was standing within inches of the gunny. Just as the man started to turn, Davis slammed his Colt into the back of the gunny's head. He was still a powerful man. The gunny stayed conscious long enough to spin half around. But by then the lawman's fist had exploded on the side of the man's face. The gun dropped to the floor and the man followed seconds later.

"We sure do appreciate it, Marshal," the bald cardplayer said. Even though he'd sounded calm when the gun was on him, his voice now sounded shaky. Sweat gleamed on his forehead. Sometimes a man didn't get scared until afterward.

"Just doin' my job, boys. But you could do me a favor by cartin' this one over to the jail and throwin' him into a cell. There'll be a deputy there to help you."

"Hell, yes, we will," the bald one said. He glanced down at the unconscious gunny. "Be our pleasure, matter of fact."

The other players voiced agreement.

Davis went back to the bar. Irish shoved a glass of beer at him.

"Thanks for letting me know about him," Davis said. "At least that's one less I have to worry about."

Irish scanned the place, making sure that business was getting back to normal. Didn't want to lose any money just because a gunny raised a little hell. Then his eyes returned to Davis. "It's the damned gold shipments. No easier way to make money than to hire some gunnies to hijack the gold."

"Yeah, and no easier way to take over somebody else's mine than by stealing all their profits." He took a deep swig of beer. Irish knew who he was talking about. Nothing more needed to be said.

"I'm your first stop?"

"Yep. Now I check out the other saloons and hotels. They're not all as cooperative as you. Easiest way to deal with gunnies is to get to them before they can

9

do anything. But to do that I need people to keep an eye out. Most folks just don't want to be bothered."

"Or they're afraid."

Davis sighed. "Yeah, I guess I forgot about poor old Millard."

Ab Millard had run a saloon a block down Main Street. He'd sent a runner telling the lawman that a drifter who looked a lot like a gunny was doing some drinking and bragging in his saloon. Davis showed up and arrested the man without incident. He held him for five days, then sent him packing without any guns or weapons. Unfortunately, this particular gunny held a grudge. Three days after his release, now armed, he snuck back into town and killed poor Ab for cooperating with Davis.

"Glad you killed that little bastard when you caught him, Marshal," Irish said bitterly. "If you hadn't, I would've."

And Davis reckoned he would have at that.

"Thank the heavens you were with us today," Walt said to Fargo as he and two others piled the bodies on a tarp on top of the gold boxes in the wagon. Fargo and another man had already rounded up the robbers' horses. It looked like Cain was not only going to get his gold into Sacramento, he was going to gain some nice horses for his stable.

"You men would have done all right against these idiots," Fargo said as he dismounted. Then he turned to Cain. "You recognize any of this gear or the horses?"

Cain shook his head. "None of it, but they don't go with these men. At least the four miners."

"Noticed that, huh?"

Cain laughed. "Yeah. Don't miss a detail, do I?"

Fargo glanced around at the other guards. "Anyone recognize any of these jokers or the horses?"

One of the guards said he might know one of the men, but he wasn't sure. He thought he'd seen him in town, and he more than likely worked for another mine in the Placerville area. He didn't know which one though.

No help at all.

But it made sense that Cain and his men didn't know the robbers. The Placerville area had exploded in size to a small city, and the men working in each mine tended to stay together and drink together and not mix much with others from other mines. The mine owners liked it that way as well and tended to demand as much loyalty out of their men as they dared.

What Fargo wanted to know was how men from another mine knew when Cain was planning an ore shipment into town. There was a leak in Cain's organization, and Fargo intended to plug it, more than likely with lead. But bringing up that subject standing in the hot sun with dead bodies in the wagon and guards listening didn't seem like a good idea.

Fargo had the wagon wait twenty minutes before starting back up to give himself time to scout ahead. But he didn't find any problems, and they reached Sacramento just before sunset.

They dropped the bodies off with the undertaker and reported in to the marshal, then took care of the gold ore. After that, Cain got rooms for his men in a boarding house on the edge of town and stabled all the horses together. Cain and Fargo had to take rooms in a cheap hotel because the expensive hotel was all booked up.

Fargo's room was being cleaned when he reached it. He saw a slim but shapely bottom clothed in blue gingham as a young woman was bent over the bed tugging the covers into place. When she heard him and faced him, he saw she had the freckle-faced prettiness of a lot of pioneer girls.

"I'm just about done here," she said in a sweet little voice.

"No hurry," Fargo said. "It's a pleasure to watch you work."

She blushed but then allowed herself a tiny smile. "Well, that's not a very polite thing to say, but I appreciate it."

Fargo dumped his saddlebags in a corner and surveyed the room. Not that there was much to see. One cheap hotel room was the same as another no matter where you were. Bed, chair, bureau, washbasin, pitcher. It was a step up from a prison cell and a step down from where respectable folks stayed. At that he had to laugh at himself. That was one of the few things he'd never been called—respectable.

"My name's Fargo. What's yours?" he asked her as she moved to dust off the bureau.

"Sally DeWitt. My uncle owns this hotel."

The sunlight streaming through the window made her reddish blond hair glow. The deep blue eyes glowed too. He watched the rise and fall of her fetching breasts. He felt himself stir in a pleasant way.

He crossed the room to the bed. He sat down and began to pull his boots off. He was pleased to see her come over to him. "Here, I can get those off for you."

"Part of the service?"

This time she didn't blush. This time, unspoken, she'd clearly decided that she was as intrigued with him as he was with her.

"I do this for just about everybody, actually. My uncle says guests come back if we kind of coddle them a bit."

He stuck his right leg out and she pulled his boot off. She was close enough that he could smell the natural perfumes of her body, of her hair. It was difficult to keep from grabbing her.

Left foot. She leaned over, slid his boot off. But this time, whether by accident or design, she lost her balance momentarily and started to pitch forward.

Right into Fargo's arms. He held her there for a moment. Her face was so close, her lips so ripe, he didn't want to let her go. She must have shared the same feeling because she gently pushed him back on the bed, her open mouth on his even before his spine touched the covers.

She was no innocent, which pleased him. She quickly found the buttons on his trousers and brought forth the stern proof of his desire. She put her lips to it and made him twist and gasp in pleasure. No innocent at all. She knew exactly what she was doing.

He rolled on his side so that while she was bringing him to even greater need, he was able to unbutton the back side of her dress. As he'd suspected, she was naked beneath. Now it was his turn to push her flat on the bed. Her turn to twist and gasp in pleasure as his mouth found the pink nubs of her nipples and his fingers found the hot dampness of her sex. Her hips began to wriggle as his finger found her most sensitive spot. Her breath came in warm bursts. He wanted to move his face down her body but she stopped him moments later. Her own fingers found him, made him even more needful of her. She guided him up into her, giving a small cry when he was fully in her. A cry of both pleasure and pain because of his size.

They made love as if they were participating in an intricate dance, tiny, expert thrusts and touches and shifting positions. The dance became increasingly frenzied, his hands clutching her buttocks, her fingers clawing his back with such urgency that it was as if she wanted his entire body inside her.

Then her legs were up over his shoulders and he was riding both of them home. Deeper and deeper he drove as she clung to him with a desperation that bordered on madness. And then he felt her entire body lurch with great, profound, overwhelming pleasure as she began thrashing left, thrashing right in completion. And he was only thirty seconds right behind her.

They lay, temporarily exhausted, on the bed in silence until Fargo said: "I can see why your guests keep coming back."

"You're the only guest I've ever done it with. The

13

others are—" She didn't finish the sentence. She didn't need to. Fargo had seen for himself the shabby drinkers and broken-down criminal types who were sitting in the lobby when he came in.

She touched him, found he was getting ready for more. "Darn."

"What?"

"I have to get back to work."

"You couldn't just—"

"Afraid not. If my uncle doesn't see me for fifteen minutes, he comes looking for me. And this would be a little awkward." She grinned and kissed him on the nose.

Then, with amazing speed and grace, she got up off the bed and into her clothes.

"You tell your uncle I'll definitely come back," Fargo said as she opened the door. She left him with a girlish giggle.

Since last time Fargo had been there, Sacramento had settled into the feeling of a large city. It was nestled along the edge of the Sacramento River and the place often had the smell of the river floating among the buildings. Not only were there a lot of two-story buildings now, but many were made of stone and brick instead of wood. The town was starting to gain a level of respectability, even with the thousands of miners who poured in and out of the area every day.

He was particularly interested in a gilded, imposing hotel called the Gold Strike. A liveried coachman helped a rich lady from a hansom cab. A doorman in a foppish military coat gave instructions to a Negro worker. A fat man in a cape, dark suit, and spats stood on the front steps looking around imperiously as if he owned all he saw.

It had been a long time since Fargo had seen a hotel like this one. He decided to go inside.

The lobby of the Gold Strike had a high ceiling, plush furniture that Fargo thought looked uncomfortable, and a carved-wood banister that ran up a grand staircase to the right of the front desk. Fargo glanced up the steps to see a stunning woman in an emerald linen dress descend the stairs.

She had freshly scrubbed skin that glowed almost pink, dark eyes, pitch-black hair, and a body that shouted to be looked at, especially with her bosom pressed upward by the tightness of the dress.

And did she know how to move, taking every step down the staircase slowly as if showing off her features to a crowd, even though Fargo knew he was the only one looking.

He didn't mind being an audience of one. He could appreciate a woman's beauty just as much as the next man, and this woman had beauty to spare. So he just stared, letting the faint click of her heels on the staircase lull him into her charms.

She smiled at him as she neared the bottom of the steps, but the smile didn't reach her eyes. That was enough to send his warning bells ringing and snap him out of the enjoyment of watching a beautiful woman.

He had always believed that the real beauty in a woman was in her eyes. Sure, beautiful bodies helped, but what showed in the eyes was what mattered.

He was still watching her when he heard a familiar voice behind him. "I was right behind you in the street. You and that cleaning gal made a lot of noise." Cain's grizzled laugh spoke of tobacco and whiskey.

As the woman neared them, she glanced at Cain and seemed to stutter in her perfect stride just slightly. She recovered quickly, but her eyes seemed to take on a level of anger Fargo wanted nothing to do with, even though her overall expression never changed. The woman would be deadly in a poker game if you didn't have a read on her and had fallen for her ample, mostly exposed charms.

At that moment Cain glanced up. "Miss Brant," he said, nodding slightly.

Fargo could tell that his old friend had no love for this woman. Hatred seemed to come closer to the emotion dripping from his words.

"Mr. Parker," she said, nodding and stopping beside the desk, staying one step up on the staircase as if to keep the upper hand in the conversation. "It is a *surprise* to see you here."

Cain said nothing, ignoring her and turning to Fargo. He cursed under his breath loudly enough for the woman to hear him. Then Cain walked away.

The woman ignored the snub as if expecting it. She put out her hand to Fargo. "Sarah Brant. I don't think I've had the pleasure."

Fargo knew a seductive look in a woman when he saw one, and this woman had the look going like a lighthouse trying to light up a foggy night. He took her offered hand, not really enjoying the moistness of her skin. He nodded slightly while looking into the dark pools of her eyes. "Skye Fargo."

"The Trailsman?" she said, yanking her hand away like she'd touched a hot stove. Now the surprise at seeing Cain had turned to worry in those dark, soulless eyes.

Fargo smiled. "Some people call me that. Some call me other names."

"Are you *working* for Cain now, Mr. Fargo?" she asked, her voice cold and low with clear disgust.

"He's my friend," Fargo said. "My *close* friend."

Her fair skin seemed to pale even further. With only a glance at Cain, she stepped down off the staircase and headed for the front door, no longer moving slowly. The way she was stomping, her dress was going to be lucky to hold her bosom in place.

"Nice meeting you, Miss Brant," Fargo said to the back of her head and her swishing dress, holding his laughter until she slammed the front door behind her.

Fargo turned back to his friend. "I see you have a way with women. Some history there?" Fargo knew that Cain's wife, Sharon, had been dead for ten years now. The man deserved to move on, but he hoped not with a woman like that one.

"That's not a woman," Cain said. "That's pure rattlesnake, the daughter of Henry Brant, the owner of

16

the mine around the ridge from Sharon's Dream. And from what I hear, she's my son's fiancée."

Now it was Fargo's turn to be surprised. "You haven't been talking to Daniel?"

The last time Fargo had seen Cain and Daniel, the kid had been maybe fifteen. He and his dad had been trying to get a mine started.

"Not for six months, since he tangled up with that thing," Cain said, nodding at the door where Sarah Brant had gone. "She poisoned him against me and Sharon's Dream and now he's working for the Brants."

"No wonder she was surprised to see you," Fargo said.

"She shouldn't have been," Cain said, shrugging. "She knows I stay in Sacramento after every gold shipment." Then he said: "And her old man's been hiring gunnies like Mick Rule to help him."

Mick Rule, Fargo thought. Gunnies didn't come any meaner than Mick Rule. But Fargo said nothing as they headed back to their hotel. There was no doubt she had been genuinely surprised to see Cain. And that could mean only one thing. This time she hadn't expected him to make it to Sacramento with his gold.

Fargo wasn't certain, but he had a hunch now which stable those horses had come from. And who had hired those men. But with Cain's son working for them, he just wouldn't let himself believe that yet.

At least not until he had a little chat with Daniel.

Daniel Parker sighted, then pitched his horseshoe. The shot was bad enough that the two men he was playing with laughed even while the shoe was in midair.

Daniel swore, shook his head. Ned Hughes snorted. "You don't have no concentration, kid. That's your problem."

Bill Peck grinned. "It's all that lovin' he's getting from the Brant woman. Can't think of nothing else."

Hughes and Peck were some more of Brant's hired

guns. Every time things quieted down, they set up for
horseshoes. Now they played in a patch of grass that
ran between two birch trees. The Brant mine was
down the hill. They always played for money but
never for much, so Daniel joined in. He'd always con-
sidered himself good at the game but in recent days
he'd played badly. Maybe they were right. Maybe it
was Sarah and how much she'd changed him.

And how much she'd confused him.

His old man had never had money till lately. Like
too many others in this state, his father could have
turned outlaw. That was a much easier way to make
money than honest labor. But the old man never did.
And he spent his time with his son trying to persuade
the boy to follow the same lawful path.

"Hey, your throw again," Hughes said. "Lessen
you're off with your lady somewhere."

Both Hughes and Peck laughed. But it was just josh-
ing. No mean intent. A lot of the other gunnies made
sarcastic remarks about how a beautiful woman like
that could sure do a lot better than Daniel. He knew
they were jealous but that didn't make their comments
any easier to take. Hughes and Peck were older. They
seemed more tolerant of Daniel and his situation.

Daniel forced a smile. "Hang on to your money,
boys. Just you watch this."

He took his time. He sighted carefully. He almost
threw but then stopped himself. He didn't really care
what they thought of his playing. It was himself he
wanted to impress. He wanted to feel he was in control of his life again. Being with a woman like Sarah
and turning bad had completely changed him. He felt
different now and he wasn't sure if that was a good
thing or not. He wished thoughts of his old man would
leave him alone. He knew what his father would think
of what he was doing.

"You did it again, kid." This time Hughes's laugh
had an edge to it. "Your mind started driftin' away
again. Now you want to play this game or not?"

And damned if it wasn't true. One moment he'd

been concentrating on throwing a masterful pitch, and the next his attention was wrenched away to mull his situation again. It was worse than being drunk.

He grinned. People liked his grin. "I was just thinkin' about how I'm gonna embarrass you two with this one." He held up the iron shoe for them to see. "You ready?"

"We're ready," Peck said. "But are you?"

This time Daniel made quick work of it. He took careful aim, angled his elbow the way he always did, and then let fly.

The horseshoe rose in the air and then began its descent. A soft mountain breeze cooled Daniel's face as he watched it. And then came the *clink*, the satisfying sound of victory.

"Well, looks like the kid's got his brain back," Hughes said.

The playing went smoothly from then on. Hughes and Peck were good at it but Daniel was better. But he could tell that they appreciated the competition. He was uncomfortable around gunnies—maybe you got used to people who killed in cold blood after you'd done it a few times yourself—but these two didn't brag and threaten the way the others did. They might have been his uncles.

The game was winding down when a stout man came uptrail and stood there for a time watching them. He looked amused. Hughes saw him first. He said, "Well, if it isn't Mr. Brant himself."

Peck and Daniel now turned to face Brant. None of the gunnies liked the man. He was too cold, too arrogant. Even killers liked a little friendliness in their relationships.

"Hell of a way to waste your lives," Brant said.

"You a preacher now, are you, Brant?" Hughes snapped. "Tell us how to spend our time."

"I believe in bettering your lot. That's why people came west. To improve their lot. And you don't do that by pitching horseshoes all day."

"Yeah." Peck laughed. "We should be fritterin' our

time away in whorehouses. That'd be better now, wouldn't it, Mr. Brant?"

Daniel was surprised at how openly sarcastic the gunnies were around Brant. He might be their boss in the short term but their guns made them more powerful and more dangerous than he could ever be no matter how much money he had. For Brant it had to be like keeping panthers on a leash. He just had to hope they never slipped that leash and attacked him.

"You probably had a halfway decent reason for comin' up here, Brant," Hughes said. He winked at Peck. "Maybe you'd like to share it with us."

Brant shook his head in disgust. Locally he was a man who brooked no insolence. Townspeople feared him financially and his mine guards physically. But these drifters, these lowborn killers, they had no respect for who Brant was—or at least who he planned to be after he took things over around here.

"I want to have a meeting down at the mine. And I want you down there."

"I hope it doesn't run as long as that last meeting," Peck said. "I damned near went to sleep."

Brant's face flushed deep red. He looked out of place up here in his city suit. Out of place and at the moment completely at the mercy of the mocking men he badly needed right now. "I'll expect you along in ten minutes. And not one minute later."

He turned and tromped back down the hill.

Hughes and Peck ridiculed Brant, of course. Daniel made a good audience. His laughter was deep and genuine.

But as the jokes kept coming, he thought how strange his life had become. A man hires you and you make fun of him. And he hires you to kill other people.

Yes, indeed. How strange Daniel Parker's life had become.

2

You don't just bring dead bodies into a town without there being some questions asked. The next morning, the inquest with the marshal in front of a magistrate took less than a half hour, with Cain and one of his men giving their side of the story after Fargo gave his. They were all cleared and the judge actually thanked them for taking care of the problem.

Fargo had no doubt that this gang of thieves wasn't the main problem. More than likely, by getting rid of them, he was going to force Brant into hiring more experienced and dangerous men to go after Cain's gold.

After dinner the night before, Fargo had asked around and it seemed that no one recognized the men lying in coffins in the morgue, and no one had inquired about their horses or their gear. He hadn't expected anyone to, but it never hurt to ask.

Outside the stone courthouse, on the edge of the dusty street, Marshal Davis stopped Cain and Fargo. He stood about the same height as Fargo, slightly taller than Cain, and looked like he would be a formidable foe in a fight, even though gray was touching his hair on the sides. He had on a black suit jacket and a wide-brimmed hat. The matching Colts that the marshal carried comfortably in leather on his hips told Fargo the man could shoot with both hands, probably with deadly accuracy. And from what Fargo had heard about Marshal Davis, the man was harsh but fair, and kept the streets of Sacramento pretty much under control.

"Fargo," the marshal said, staring directly into Fargo's eyes. "It's been a pleasure meeting you. You mind? I got a question for you."

"Fire away, Marshal. Not sure I have an answer, but I'll do my darnedest."

Marshal Davis smiled. "Are you working the Placerville road for Mr. Parker?"

"I am," Fargo said.

Cain laughed. "Thank all the heavens that he is. It would be me and my men lying in that morgue without him helping me out."

Marshal Davis nodded. "Glad you're on the job. I need all the help I can get on that road with all the robberies going on and the amount of gold being transported into town. And from the looks of them, I doubt these men are the main problem."

"I have the same hunch," Fargo said.

Cain laughed again and slapped Fargo on the back. "I trust your hunches, Skye. You're the only one who can get my shipments through. They're the ones that seem to be getting attacked the most."

"I've noticed that as well," Marshal Davis said. "That's why I'm glad Fargo is with you. That alone should cut down on some of the problems on that road. Your reputation precedes you, sir."

"Yeah, I've noticed that," Fargo said. "Kind of like a bad smell."

Placerville had expanded down a valley and spread out like an ugly weed over the hillsides. Tents, shacks, and lean-tos surrounded the two-story buildings that formed the town's core. Mine tailings dotted the hills like scars in all directions and there wasn't a tree in sight left standing.

By the time Fargo left Cain at his mine and rode into town, it was getting close to dark. The heat of the day still hovered over the buildings, keeping everything feeling dusty and tight.

Cain had been hoping that Fargo would stay with him in his big, empty house, but Fargo had declined, saying it just wasn't his style. Cain had laughed and said he knew that, but had to offer. Then Cain had suggested that Fargo stay in the nicest hotel in town and put it on his tab. Fargo intended to take him up on his offer. While he preferred sleeping on the trail, he wasn't about to turn down an occasional hotel and well-cooked food.

The Wallace Hotel filled a corner and part of one block of the boomtown. It had been built with rough stone and painted wood, with large windows and a covered wooden porch and sidewalk area that wrapped around the big building. On one street was the entrance to the saloon; around the corner on the other street was the entrance to the hotel.

Fargo went in the hotel entrance and looked around. The hotel had a lobby that was separate from the saloon, and like the hotel in Sacramento, there was a grand staircase made out of marble and polished wood that soared upward in a wide curve over the stuffed chairs and couches of the lobby.

There was a separate dining area off of the lobby and a door that marked the entrance into the saloon and kept the noise in the lobby down. The smells coming from the dining area were inviting and Fargo set his mind on a good dinner, then maybe a little poker and a drink to round off the evening.

He arranged for a bath to be drawn in his room as he checked in. Before going upstairs, Fargo poked his head in to the saloon to take a look around. The place had a number of what looked like high-stakes poker games going and a stage for dancers later in the evening. It smelled of cigar smoke and whiskey and felt inviting. A brass spittoon sat near every table and behind the long wooden bar. The wall was full of bottles arranged around a huge ornate mirror. Fargo had no doubt he could spend many a comfortable evening in the place.

He was about to head to his room when a woman

in a dark dress with pink trim stepped into the saloon from a back room. She had long brown hair, beautiful white skin, and green eyes that could hold a man firmly in place no matter what the occasion. Fargo knew that for a fact, since he had spent many a pleasurable night staring into those eyes in Colorado a few years before.

Her name was Anne Dowling, and she was the widow of Wallace Dowling. Wallace had been a rancher and had been killed by rustlers. Anne had run the ranch for years before Fargo met her. They had become lovers and he had helped her out with two of her ranch hands who were threatening her and trying to take over her ranch.

Her bubbling personality made her one of those people whom it was almost impossible to say no to. And she had been a lover like none he had known since.

Fargo stared, taking in her beauty and flowing movements as she headed behind the bar like she owned the place. Then it dawned on him that likely she did. This was the Wallace Hotel. Her husband had been named Wallace.

He moved through the saloon, watching her work on something on the back counter. He finally reached the bar and stood staring at the white skin of her neck above the collar of her dress. He had loved the feel of her skin. The memory was as if they had made love yesterday, not four years before.

The bartender approached him. "What will it be, sir?"

"A simple hello from a beautiful woman would be a nice start."

The bartender frowned and started to say something when Anne spun around, all smiles. "Skye!"

She moved to the bar, took Fargo's hands, and squeezed them, then almost climbed up on the bar to kiss his cheek.

Her green eyes sparkled with excitement at seeing

him. He had to admit, he was excited in more ways than one at seeing her again as well.

"What are you doing in Placerville?"

"I was about to ask you the same question," Fargo said, laughing.

"Long story." She squeezed his hands again, her smile beaming just as he remembered it. "Have you had dinner?"

"Just going up to my room to drop off my gear, get cleaned up, and do exactly that."

"Wonderful," she said, laughing. "Mind if a woman invites herself to your table?"

"Anne, it would be my pleasure," he said, bowing slightly.

She released her grip on his hands and turned to the bartender. "Reg, this is the Trailsman. He doesn't pay for a drink in here."

Reg smiled and nodded to Fargo, clearly recognizing the name. "Nice meeting you, sir. Anne has spoken of you often and I've heard many other stories. It is an honor and a pleasure."

"A bartender who serves me free drinks," Fargo said, shaking the bartender's solid hand and smiling. "I think the pleasure is all mine."

"Anything to keep you around a little longer," Anne said, laughing.

"Oh, I might be here awhile," Fargo said. Then, before she could ask, he said, "Long story. I'll tell you all about it over dinner. Give me thirty minutes to clean off a week's worth of trail dust for such wonderful company."

She half climbed up on the bar again and kissed his cheek for the second time. "I'll be in the dining room. Don't keep a girl waiting too long. We have a lot of catching up to do."

Then she winked and turned and headed for the back room.

Fargo watched her go, his mind filled with memories of all their nights together.

"She's quite a woman," Reg said.

"You've known her for a while then?"

"Tried to get her to marry me—that's how well I've known her." Then he smiled. "Oh, don't worry. Those days are long behind me. Mostly just my daydreams more than anything else. To her I've never been more than a friend. Sort of like a big brother. But you"— he smiled—"all she does is talk about you. Skye this and Skye that. She has her own daydreams when it comes to you."

"Well, I've had a few about her too."

"You don't strike me as the settling-down kind."

"No. I'm not. But once in a while she makes it very tempting. All these years go by and I still think of her. Then I run into her—"

Reg had to move down the bar to serve a pair of new customers. He was a burly, quiet gent, one of those men whose presence had a calming effect on people. A real asset in the bartending business, especially given the nature of Western saloons, where fights were as common as beers. Fargo imagined that when a brawl broke out Reg had two weapons—the ball bat behind the bar and his own assertive presence.

When Reg came back, he said, "You've probably noticed we've got a lot of crazy people running around these streets of ours."

"Gold?"

Reg nodded. "Sort of ugly what gold does to people. You take a nice, decent feller everybody trusts— he gets a little gold and suddenly he sees everybody as his enemy. He's got to protect the gold. I've seen it over and over. Works the same way from the other side too. You have two friends and one of them gets a strike and the other doesn't. The one without the strike gets jealous. A lot of time—and I've seen this happen too—he gets so jealous that some night he's all drunked up and he kills his old friend in cold blood. That's the kind of effect gold has on people."

"And then you've got one mine owner trying to take over another mine owner."

"That's what's going on around here. Already been a lot of men killed. The more gold, the more killing." He laughed. "That's why I'm happy to stay behind the bar here and mind my own business."

Reg had to serve a few more customers. Fargo looked around the place. Lamps were lowered over poker tables. A man in a funny little hat and red sleeve garters was sitting down to play the piano. Three men at one table were rolling dice.

Boomtown. You'd find men here from Europe, from Asia. All trying to get rich. Reg was right. Otherwise decent, reasonable, realistic men would leave their homes and families to come west to search for gold. And when they got out here, something happened to them. They changed, no longer decent, reasonable, or realistic. Too many of them changed into hungry wolves.

Reg came back. "This probably sounds kind of crazy, giving advice to the Trailsman. But this is one of those towns where it's hard to know who to trust. I want Anne to be happy. I doubt she'll get you to the altar but she's got a chance as long as nobody turns you into a corpse. So just watch yourself. I don't want to see that little gal disappointed."

This time when Reg went down the bar, there was an air of sadness about him. Fargo figured that despite his earlier words, the man was still painfully in love with Anne. It must have been hard for him to talk to Fargo about the woman he loved—the woman who loved Fargo and not him.

But Reg was one of those rare people—he put the wishes and needs of his friend Anne above his own wishes and needs.

Anne was lucky to have a friend like Reg.

Fargo hadn't enjoyed himself this much in a long time. The steak cooked exactly the way he liked it, the potato soft and moist, the waiters around only when needed. But it was the company of Anne that made the meal memorable.

27

After they had eaten, they talked far into the night over fine wine, far after the restaurant was closed to the regular guests.

As he had guessed, she was the owner of the hotel. She had sold her ranch after one rough winter and headed west, ending up here with enough money and the right timing to build Placerville's largest and nicest hotel and saloon. She hadn't remarried and had no intention to.

"You spoiled me, Fargo," she said at one point, putting her hand on his and looking into his eyes. "Not only for other men, but you showed me that there was more to living than just a ranch and cattle."

"So, are you happy here?"

"More than I ever thought possible," she said. "Sure, I have my problems, but I also have far more good days than bad. And this place is a gold mine without having to lift a shovel."

"And what happens if the mines start to play out?" Fargo asked. He couldn't begin to count the number of towns that had boomed and then vanished into dust over the years when the gold or silver ran out. Or the railway passed the town by. Or the water went bad.

"I've been watching," she said, her eyes and expression serious for the first time in the conversation. "If it starts to look like it's going to dry up, I'll sell out quickly and Reg and I and a dozen others who came with me from Colorado will move to another city, build another place, and start again."

"You've sure got a good friend in Reg."

"I sure do," Anne said. "He took over as ranch foreman after you left. He's now my hotel manager, the person I trust to run this place. He's almost my business partner. He designed this place and helped build it. He gets a share of the profits as well."

"He still loves you, you know."

Anne looked directly into his eyes. "And I'm still in love with you."

Someday down the road, if he ever got too old for

28

moving around, Anne might be the one he would come back to. But he wasn't that old yet, and she knew that.

"So," Anne said, sipping her wine and sitting back, "what's this long story that brought you to Placerville?"

He told her everything, including what had happened on the Placerville road yesterday.

She nodded, even though there was worry in her eyes. "Cain is a good man. Very well respected around here. He treats his men well and plays fair. It makes sense he would be your friend. But some of these other mine owners you want to stay clear of."

"I'd be grateful for any local knowledge I can get," Fargo said.

Then he leaned forward and lowered his voice just to make sure no one could hear, even though the dining area seemed clear and their table candles were the only ones still burning in the room. "What do you know of Henry Brant?"

Anne looked disgusted at the very mention of the name. "The worst of the worst. And his daughter is as bad as they come as well. I won't even allow his men to drink or eat in here. He's known to play poker over at the Benson Saloon. I hear Cain's son is mixed up with the daughter. Doesn't seem right to me."

"I heard that too," Fargo said.

"So why the hushed tone and the question?" Anne asked.

Fargo told her about his brief meeting with Sarah Brant, and then about the horses and gear that the robbers had been using. "It doesn't add up completely, but it sure points a finger."

"And I wouldn't put it past the Brants to be behind the robbery attempts on Cain's shipments," Anne said. Then she too lowered her voice to a whisper. "There are rumors that the Brants' mine has mostly played out and they're working underground toward Cain's tunnels that are still hitting vein. But they're only rumors and there's no way of proving it until something happens underground and Brant breaks through into one of Cain's tunnels."

Fargo nodded. "It wouldn't be the first time there's been a war between mines underground."

After another half hour of talking business, Anne stood and stretched. "It's getting late and a lady like me needs her beauty sleep."

Fargo could feel the disappointment hit his stomach as he stood. He had hoped for another ending to this evening.

Anne smiled at Fargo and pulled him closer to her. He was a good foot taller than she was and she pressed in close and looked up at him, her eyes twinkling. She smelled great and he could feel her ample breasts pressing into him as a reminder of good times in the past.

"To really get my beauty sleep, I could use a *good* man to tuck me in."

"I'll be as *good* as I can be," he said.

She eased up on tiptoe to kiss him. "I'm counting on that."

She took him by the hand and led him through the kitchen to the back staircase. Only a dishwasher was still at work and he didn't look up as they passed. Her room was an unmarked door at the end of the hallway, about five doors down from his room. She let him in.

A large dresser and mirror filled one wall beside an oversized white bathtub. A huge bed with an ornate headboard was against another wall, and a large closet led off to one side of the dresser. There was also a comfortable-looking reading chair between two corner windows and a stand with a number of books on it beside the chair. Drapes had been pulled across the two windows and the only light in the room came from a lantern turned low on the nightstand.

She had gone from a large sprawling ranch house in Colorado to this room, and yet this room felt as comfortable to him as her house had been. It seemed that anywhere Anne lived, he felt at home.

She locked and bolted the door, then with a rush was in his arms.

"Skye, I can't tell you how much I've thought of you," she said breathlessly between passionate kisses.

Fargo didn't lie when he said he had thought about her a lot as well. And right now his body was responding to her as she pressed against him, rubbing up and down with every kiss.

Finally, during one long kiss, he swept her off her feet and carried her to her large feather bed, easing her down onto the beautiful pink satin quilt that covered the sheets. Then he slowly undressed her, kissing every new inch of exposed soft skin until she finally lay there naked and panting.

He stood and began peeling off his clothes, never taking his gaze from her.

Her beauty took his breath away. Her large nipples heaved up and down with every breath, just begging to be kissed again and again. Her stomach was flat and firm, almost like a much younger woman's would be, but her wider hips showed her longer years. He loved every detail of her, from her soft hair to her tiny feet.

She spread her legs, exposing herself slightly. "You are sure taking your time getting undressed," she said, her voice a hoarse whisper. She had a look in her eyes of hunger and lust. He remembered that look, that unbridled passion she always expressed toward him. That look alone had kept him thinking about her over the years.

When he shoved his pants down and his hard, thick member sprang free, she couldn't wait any longer. Before he could kick one leg out of his pants, she sat up on the edge of the bed and grabbed his manhood, licking it and playing with him.

The sensation of her kisses and her warm lips almost knocked him over before he could finally get a leg loose from his britches and get his balance.

Then, suddenly, she stopped and pulled him down on top of her.

With a quick, experienced hand, she directed him inside her moist tunnel.

He filled her up completely and she gasped.

All he wanted to do was lay there for a moment, memorizing the feeling of being inside her. But she would have none of that.

She moved under him, forcing him to move.

He raised himself up on his arms so he wasn't crushing her and so that he could see her beautiful face in the dim light from the bedside lamp. She had her eyes closed and a pink flush filled every inch of her face and soft skin.

She moved slowly at first as he held himself there, grinding her hips up and down into his, taking him completely one moment, then almost losing him the next.

Finally, he let himself join her movements, and together they slowly picked up speed. The expression on her face gained intensity and her movements became more demanding.

He leaned down and buried his face in her soft brown hair and the smooth skin on her neck as he pushed back against her.

Like a locomotive building up steam, they went faster and faster, never seeming to miss a beat, always in unison, holding each other in all ways.

It felt so perfect, so intense, that there was no holding either of them back and they both reached their peaks in hard, fast, flesh-slapping unison.

Fargo couldn't remember being so out of breath before. Somehow, he managed to ease up on one elbow to watch Anne gasp for breath as well, her chest heaving up and down, her body still clamped tight around his manhood.

There had been a number of special women in his life, but none like this woman under him now. Everything about her filled him with the desire to stay with her, even though he knew he wouldn't. But maybe this job with Cain and the miners might last a while, give them some real time together.

Anne opened one eye and squinted up at him. "It's

been a long time. That was better than I remembered it."

He kissed her and smiled. "Yeah, and a great dessert after a great meal."

She opened the other eye and stared at him. "Who said anything about dessert there, mister? That was just the appetizer."

With that, she pushed him over sideways and without losing him inside her, she rode up on top of him, settling down on his manhood like a rider settling into a saddle.

He could feel himself responding, filling her up as he again grew into the task at hand.

"You got yourself a really hungry woman here," she said, smiling down at him as her long hair framed her face like a beautiful picture. "Let's work on the main course before we talk about dessert."

"Just don't expect a seven-course meal," he said, smiling at her.

She laughed, then slowly moved on him, up and down, easing herself along his shaft, letting the juices between them flow as she ground down, then lifted up again. "We'll see about that," she said, smiling that hungry, loving look he had come to like so much.

Then she picked up speed and all thought of a witty response left his head.

Fargo had just walked out of the hotel when the bullet sang past him, digging its way into the wood of a slender pillar. Behind him a woman in the lobby screamed as a second bullet smashed through the glass of the front door. By this time Fargo was in a crouch with his gun drawn. Even in a town as rough as this one, gunfire on Main Street alarmed everybody.

He got a glimpse of the gunman just before the man disappeared behind the false front of the general store across the street. Fargo should have been easy pickings. But given all the street traffic—wagons, buggies, as well as people—it was probably difficult to kill Fargo without risking killing somebody else.

A small crowd started to form immediately. The hotel lobby was filled with shouting, cursing people who made it sound as though the earth was coming to an end. You'd expect more control from people who lived in a mining town.

But Fargo's only concern now was getting the gunman. He pushed his way through the people who'd stopped in the middle of the street to see what was going on. He knew he had only a minute or two to find his man. The shooter would have a horse waiting for him. He'd be in the saddle as soon as he worked his way down off the flat roof of the general store.

Fargo was almost across the street and ready to run to the alley that divided the general store from the druggist's when somebody shouted, "Look out, mister!"

Fargo heard the horse before he saw him. And when he saw him he realized that the gunman wasn't his only problem. Something had spooked the big animal. No surprise after gunfire and all the calamity in the street. Horses weren't any different from humans in that respect. When they got scared, their natural instinct was to flee. And that's what this bucking, whinnying animal was trying to do.

The girl riding the paint was now as spooked as the horse, trying to bring it under control. Fargo moved away from the hooves of the animal so that he was in no danger, but he couldn't just let the young girl get thrown off and hurt.

Fargo knew a trick a wise Virginian stable owner had once taught him. When you're dealing with a spooked horse, the fastest and surest way to get it unspooked is to grab the reins and force it to point its head down. Most spooked horses have their heads raised to the sky. Lowering the head calms the animal and takes its attention away from whatever spooked him.

Fargo ran to the girl. She was screaming for help. All her confidence in handling her horse was gone. All that was left was fear. Every time the animal bucked she screamed louder. Fargo's first instinct had been to shout his instructions to the girl. But he could see she was too panicked to hear him.

He reached up and grabbed the reins himself. He pulled on them firmly and said, "Calm down, boy; calm down." The girl kept on screaming, which didn't help a whole hell of a lot.

But after keeping his hand on the reins and repeating, "Calm down, boy," several times, the paint began to respond enough that Fargo could grab the girl and lower her to the ground while keeping control of the animal.

Fargo patted the horse's neck and continued speaking to him in a soothing voice. Head lowered, breathing starting to sound normal again, the paint became the trustworthy family horse it usually was.

The onlookers were impressed. He felt many pats on his back and shoulders. The young girl was crying but thanking him over and over. Two or three men offered to buy him a drink.

Fargo's attention was fixed on the general store across from him. The gunman would be long gone. But he might have left some clues about his identity.

Fargo walked into the general store. The various smells were intoxicating. New denim, leather, licorice, tobacco, flour—no wonder the old ones liked to sit in general stores and play checkers all day.

The small Swede in the rimless glasses behind the counter said, "I seen it all, mister. Them shots somebody took at you, I mean. And I want you to know I didn't have nothing to do with it. We was workin' on the roof the last couple days and left a ladder in back. That's what the sonofabitch used and I want you to know I'm sorry."

"Good enough." The Swede had answered Fargo's first question. No complicity. The gunman had used the roof because of its location directly across from the hotel. And he'd even had a little help, a ladder left innocently against the back of the store. "I guess I'll check out the roof myself."

"I sure hope you catch him, friend. This town's got

enough troubles without people shootin' at people right here on Main Street."

The roof wasn't any help in figuring out who the shooter had been. He'd been smart enough to take his shells and whether on purpose or not his boot prints were lost in the boot prints of many other men. Fargo stood in the position the gunman had taken. He had to change his mind about the prowess of the man. Even given all the street traffic, killing Fargo should have been an easy task. Fargo had paused on the top of four steps. Easy to see day or night. One shot should have killed him. Two should have made sure the job was done properly. But the man had missed both times.

Fargo walked to the back edge of the roof. Escape had been easy. A prairielike stretch of grass behind the store led to a stretch of deep timber. No problem losing yourself in there.

Fargo wondered who'd hired the man. He had a pretty good guess. Fargo grinned. He'd probably paid a fair amount of money for the shooter. But he sure hadn't gotten his money's worth.

3

For the next few days, Fargo alternated between Cain's mine, the poker tables in the Wallace saloon, and Anne's soft feather bed and loving touch. He saw his own room only once a day to shave and clean up, but since Cain was paying for it, he didn't much care.

One morning Fargo crawled out of Anne's warm bed and into the cool, early-morning air.

"Where are you heading, mister?" she asked, rolling over and exposing one naked breast. Her nipple hardened like a greeting to him.

Somehow he managed to keep dressing. "Got some scouting to do around Sharon's Dream."

She pulled the sheet up and covered herself just a little as she sat up more. "You expecting a fight?"

"Never know," Fargo said. "I hope not."

She nodded. "As long as you're safe. Now I'm going back to sleep for a while." She slid down and covered herself completely. "Take care."

He finished dressing and leaned over and kissed her, but she was already asleep.

On a map out at the mine, Cain showed him the claim line between Sharon's Dream and the Brant mine. It ran right up the ridgeline farther than Fargo had wanted to hike.

The sunlight was slowly working its way down the high peaks when he started up the ridgeline above the Sharon's Dream mine entrance. He had a hunch how the robbers were pinpointing Cain's shipments. He just had to confirm that hunch.

It was still an hour before Cain would normally start packing an ore wagon, so if anyone was watching, they would be up there now.

Fargo moved silently, working his way around the hill slightly and onto Brant's property so that he wouldn't be seen by anyone watching the Sharon's Dream side.

He heard the two men before he found their camp. They were muttering to each other about the cold and one of them was wishing he could start a fire.

"And bring a dozen of Cain's men up here?" the other man said.

"I know, I know," the one who had been complaining said.

"Bring a blanket tomorrow," the other man said. "I'm tired of you complaining every day."

Fargo eased up on them, moving silently, his Colt in his hand.

They were sitting on the ground under a large stone outcropping high on the ridge. From where they sat, it was only a few steps to a ledge that looked over Cain's mine and the area where the gold was loaded. More than likely every morning before sunrise these two men climbed up here and waited for any sign of the gold being loaded. They weren't miners—Fargo was sure of that. They both looked trail experienced and had guns in leather on their hips.

As Fargo watched, one of them moved forward and then, on his hands and knees, eased up to the edge and looked over. "Nothing yet."

"Still too early," the other man said. "Give it another hour and if there's nothing, we'll head back down."

Since shipments into Sacramento were always done during the day, and the gold loaded in the morning, the two on watch didn't have to wait much past ten on any given day.

Fargo needed to know exactly who these men were and who they were working for, even though he would bet anything at this point on Brant being behind the operation.

Fargo waited until the man was back sitting beside his friend before he stepped into the clearing, his Colt pointed at the two.

Both of them jumped and started to reach for their guns, but Fargo said, "Too early and too cold to die."

Both men froze, half up, half reaching for their guns.

"Sit back down now real slow and put your hands where I can see them."

Both men did as they were told. Now the trick would be getting information out of them.

"You men look to have a pretty easy job. Just sit up here and watch things down below."

"We earn our keep," the first man said. He stroked a red beard and watched Fargo skeptically.

"That's what I want to know about. Your 'keep.' Who's paying you to sit up here?"

"I'm not sure that's any of your business," said the bald one.

"Since I'm holdin' the gun, I'd say my business is anything I want it to be."

Red Beard shrugged, looked at his partner, then back to Fargo. "Nothin' worth getting shot over."

"Sensible," Fargo said.

"We just keep track of the comings and goings at the mine."

"The shipments, you mean."

"Who the hell are you exactly?" the bald one snapped.

"Name's Fargo."

Red Beard snorted. "Skye Fargo? Sure you are. And I'm George Washington."

"You can believe me or not. All I care about is finding out who hired you to sit on your lazy asses up here."

The bald one said, "You really Skye Fargo?"

"I'm really Skye Fargo."

39

"Well, hell," Red Beard said. "If that's the case, then I'll tell you right off. Sarah Brant hired us."

That rocked Fargo back a moment. It was not the answer he had been expecting.

"Not her father?"

This time both men shook their heads no.

"Does he know you're up here?"

Red Beard said, "We're just pickin' up some wages, Fargo. We don't ask no questions."

"They wouldn't tell us even if we asked," the bald one agreed.

"What about Daniel Parker? Does he know you're up here?"

The bald man said, "That kid is so under Sarah Brant's skirts, I doubt he knows when the sun comes up."

"Yeah, leads him around by the nose."

Hearing that about Daniel made Fargo feel disgusted, and sad for his friend Cain. Clearly, Daniel hadn't turned out to be the man Cain had hoped he would become.

"How long you two been working for Brant?"

"Three days," Red Beard said. "We met her in Sacramento and she offered us a lot of money to take down a gold ore shipment she said was being stolen from her father's rightful mining claim. She didn't say anything about going up against you."

Fargo nodded. After she had lost her last band of robbers willing to do her deeds, she had apparently decided to go for a little more talent. Fargo pointed over the edge. "Does that look like stealing from the Brant mine?"

Both men shrugged. The bald one said, "Fargo, we don't know what goes on inside those mines. We were just hired to do a job."

"Well," Fargo said, "unless you have a desire to be dead real soon, you go down the mountain, get your gear and horses, and without a word to anyone about this conversation, you both ride out hard and fast."

Both men nodded and just sat there.

Fargo stepped back and waved the Colt at them. "What are you waiting for? You have some hard riding to do and the day is still young."

Both men scrambled to their feet and took off running toward the Brant mine. Neither of them looked back.

At the main house, Cain was having lunch by the time Fargo returned from his hike, so he joined him in his big dining room where it was clear he ate most meals alone. The walls were covered in a fancy wallpaper, the wood floor polished to mirror level, and a huge glass chandelier hung over the table, sparkling in the morning light.

"So, have a great hike?" Cain asked, pointing to the tray of sandwiches for Fargo to help himself.

"A productive one," Fargo said, taking a thick beef sandwich from the tray. "I know how the robbers are pinpointing your ore shipments and who's behind it."

Cain stopped in midchew and stared at his old friend. "You're kidding."

Fargo bit into the sandwich, then, between bites and chewing, told Cain exactly what had happened, leaving out only the part about Daniel.

When he was finished, Cain slammed what was left of his sandwich down on his plate and stood, clearly very angry, as he paced near the head of the table. "It's hard to believe any woman could be that ruthless."

"I'm still not so sure her father isn't pulling the main strings," Fargo said. "I haven't met him yet, but from everything I've learned, the apple didn't fall far from the tree with her."

Cain nodded. "You're right about that. You sure those two men you scared off aren't going to say anything to Brant about what happened?"

"Yeah," Fargo said. "They were new hires and had no loyalty to the Brant woman."

"So, you think she's going to send two others up there tomorrow morning?" Cain asked.

"More than likely. Once a snake, always a snake, and her little outlook post has worked so far."

Cain asked the exact location and Fargo told him.

"Thanks, Skye. I'll take care of that problem tomorrow morning."

With that he stormed out of the dining room, leaving Fargo to finish his sandwich alone in the huge, formal room.

Fargo had no idea what Cain would do, and it was better he didn't know. That was between two mine owners and their crews. Fargo's job was on the trail.

Daniel had never lived at the mercy of a willful woman before and he didn't like it. The few girls he'd known were sweet and straightforward. If they liked you, they told you so and it was that simple. And then they *acted* like they liked you.

Daniel sat on the stump of a sawed oak, using his knife to whittle away at a small piece of a branch. Whittling usually calmed him. Usually. Right now, as he sat watching for Sarah Brant to come out of the house, he decided he needed something a lot more powerful than whittling to ease his temper and hurt feelings.

She'd charmed him into throwing in with her and her father, treating him as if they would be lovers forever. But, he was discovering, she paid attention to you when she wanted to. Otherwise it was as if you didn't exist.

Half an hour ago he'd walked up to where she'd been sitting in a chair outside the house talking to one of the hired guns. He'd approached her to ask if he could see her alone. But her cold stare and the smirk of the gunny embarrassed him. It was clear he wasn't wanted.

So now he sat about twenty yards from the house, waiting for her to come outside again. The gunny she'd been talking to had also been dismissed.

Everything was so damned confusing. He loved her—that was the terrible thing. He'd deserted his own father for her. But what was he going to get for his betrayal? Her treating him like a nuisance?

Maybe, he thought, *maybe she doesn't realize how serious I am about her.*

And then he felt better. Yes, that was it. Up till now he had enjoyed her as a lover but he'd been afraid to tell her how he felt. Maybe that would make all the difference. Maybe when she understood his feelings—

A sweet mountain breeze ruffled his hair and soothed his cheeks. He tossed the piece of branch away, closed his knife, and prepared himself to go up to her when she came out of the house again.

Then she was there. Sunlight dancing in her hair, her blue silk blouse tucked tightly into her black riding pants. Her rich body almost haughty as she stood with her hands on her hips.

He had just started to approach her when one of the other gunnies came from around the side of the house. He said something that Daniel couldn't hear. She laughed with a passion that was almost sexual. He saw her put her hand fondly on the man's arm. He'd never been jealous over a woman before and the feeling startled him. He wanted to draw down on the man, kill him. What right had this bastard to spend time with Daniel's woman?

He cleared his throat loudly enough to get their attention. Her gaze was even colder than before. The man looked at him briefly and then went back to talking to Sarah. She laughed again. Daniel didn't know if he could control himself. Rage, humiliation, pain.

The gunny stayed for five more minutes. Daniel knew how awkward he must look standing there watching them. But he felt paralyzed. He didn't want to see it—didn't want to see that she had lied to him—but he couldn't move. Couldn't turn away.

After the man was gone, Sarah turned and started back to the house. Daniel double-timed his way to her. Grabbed her roughly by the arm.

43

"You don't have time for me but you have time for them?"

"Unless you want to get slapped very hard, take your damned hand off me. And right now."

The harshness of her voice stunned him. He had the sense that she had just ended their relationship permanently. He pulled his hand away and said, "I'm sorry, Sarah. I shouldn't have done that."

"You're damned right you shouldn't have."

"I just want to say something to you."

She sighed impatiently. "Then go ahead. I need to get back inside."

"I love you."

And when she didn't say anything, simply stared at him as if he'd spoken in a language she'd never heard before, he said: "Maybe I made a mistake. Throwing in with you, Sarah. I guess I'll be heading out now."

The panic in her eyes surprised him. Now it was her hand on his arm. "Oh, Daniel. Daniel, you misunderstood me. We need to talk this over in bed. I didn't mean to hurt you. I really didn't. It's just that I have so much to do, I guess I don't realize when I'm not treating you right."

"But those two men who came up—"

She pressed herself against him, her soft breasts making his need for her almost frightening. He knew what had happened. He'd threatened to leave. He'd meant it. He hadn't known what else to say or do. But he was obviously a part of her plan and she didn't want to let him go.

In that moment, he knew that she was using him. That she didn't give a damn about him at all.

And the terrible thing was he didn't care. He'd take her on any terms he could have her.

"You won't leave me, will you, Daniel?" she said, her warm breath like a balm on his neck.

"No," he said. "No, I won't leave you."

Two days later, Cain was ready with another shipment into Sacramento.

So with a long and very tender kiss good-bye from Anne, Fargo again left her soft feather bed for the cold predawn air. Part of him regretted leaving; part of him felt good about being back on his big Ovaro stallion again, doing what he did best.

Fargo set up the guards and the wagon movement the same as the time before. He scouted ahead, watching for any activity or trap, staying wide of the road, often moving along a ridgeline above and ahead of the wagon.

After three dull hours of sitting his horse, rolling and smoking cigarettes and reliving some very pleasant memories of Anne, trouble finally struck around the middle of the afternoon.

One glance at the gunnies ready to rob the gold shipment told Fargo that the Brants had stepped up in the world. These were hardened killers, ready to do whatever was necessary to take the gold.

Ten of them.

Their plan was simple and hard to see coming. The Placerville road had a decent amount of traffic in the afternoon. Since Fargo had the gold shipment moving slowly to give him time to scout ahead, it had been passed numerous times by other wagons and men on horses.

As Fargo watched from a low ridge just over a rifle shot away, three men came riding up from behind the wagon, their rifles in sheaths, their guns on hips. They nodded hello to the men guarding the wagon and Cain even pulled the wagon slightly off to one side to let them pass.

Everything seemed fine, but Fargo had a gut sense it wasn't, so he moved a little higher so he could keep an eye on the three for a little farther down the road.

And he had been right.

The three men went on ahead, moving at a normal pace around a bend in the approaching narrow canyon. Then Fargo caught a glimpse of them stopping their horses and dismounting where the road went between two rock ledges along a mostly dry streambed not far from the wagon at all, pulling carbines from their sheaths.

Fargo glanced back at Cain. The wagon would be on the bushwhackers before Fargo could get down the hill.

Fargo grabbed his Colt and fired into the air twice to get the wagon to stop and to warn his party as he headed down through the rocks toward them as fast as he could.

Suddenly, from the direction of Placerville, seven more men appeared and rode at the wagon hard and fast, guns drawn, dust kicking up behind their horses.

Cain had heard the warning shots and then heard the men pounding down on them from behind. He directed the team and wagon off the road and into some rocks. Then he and his men took cover as the robbers burst upon them.

It sounded like a small war going on as Fargo rode hard and fast for the fight, pushing his Ovaro over the rough ground. He had his carbine out and in his hand. All he had to do was get into range.

At the same time as the men on horseback were attacking the guards and Cain, the three men who had passed the wagon moved quickly back up the road to join in. Two of them saw Fargo coming and leveled shots at him, even though he was mostly out of range.

Suddenly, something hit his shoulder, the force stunning him. The impact spun him backward and off his horse, knocking the wind out of him as he hit the ground hard, facedown.

It took him a second through the echoes of gunfire to realize he had been shot. He gasped for air as stabbing pain coursed through him.

From what he could tell, the bullet had gone through his shoulder. He'd been shot before. He knew when a wound was bad and when it wasn't. This one, if he got to a doctor soon enough, would be all right.

He ignored the pain and took the deepest breath he could to clear his head. Then he grabbed his handkerchief and stuffed it against the wound, pushing hard against the intense pain to stop the bleeding.

He grabbed the Henry that had fallen beside him and crawled up on a boulder just enough to rest the carbine and get a shot at the men below.

From the looks of it, three or four of Cain's men were still alive and fighting. Fargo couldn't tell if one of them was his friend.

Fargo took another painful breath to calm himself, then pulled off a shot at a man working his way around behind the defenders. The man went over backward and Fargo slammed another shell into the chamber.

His next target was a man on a horse. This one spun off his mount and into a large rock as Fargo's aim proved true.

Three of the robbers turned and fired at him, forcing him off the rock to get cover.

"Get the wagon," one man shouted, his voice echoing up the hill. "Let's get out of here."

Fargo poked his head back up and took another quick shot at another robber. The man slumped to the ground like someone had cut off his legs. From the rocks, Cain's other guards renewed their fire and took down another robber, but by now one man was on the wagon with the gold, heading the team down the road.

Fargo pulled off a shot at the driver, but his lead went into the buckboard seat beside the man, sending splinters flying. The driver ducked and pushed the team even harder. By the time Fargo could get another shot off, the man was out of range.

He was about to turn the Henry on one of the stragglers when he recognized him. It was Daniel, Cain's son.

Fargo couldn't believe that Daniel would rob his own father. How had the kid gone that bad that fast?

Fargo knocked the last robber beside Daniel off his horse with one last shot and let Daniel get away.

The robbery was over.

Fargo slumped to the dirt and leaned against the rock as he tried to catch his breath against the pain. This had gone wrong so fast, he couldn't believe it. He had lost the gold, and who knew how many good men were dead down there?

Suddenly he realized he hadn't seen Cain in the last few moments of that fight.

He whistled for the Ovaro, who showed up a moment later. Using his horse to steady himself as he stood, he managed to get mounted and slowly work his way down the hill, not really wanting to look at what lay ahead.

But he did.

Six of the ten bushwhackers were down. It looked like three of the six men from the mine were also down. And Fargo could see the three remaining men crouching beside a man in a red plaid shirt. Cain.

It took Fargo only a moment to get out of the rocks and to the road.

It turned out that two men were dead and Cain was seriously wounded. Fargo knelt beside his friend. Cain was out cold and his breathing was shallow from the wound in his upper chest. The men had already tried to stop the bleeding. Cain might live if they got him help.

Fargo stood, ignoring his own wound and pain.

The gold was gone. Daniel, Cain's own son, had led the attack. Why would a good kid like Daniel turn on his own father? None of this made sense.

Fargo knew what he had to do. He turned to the three surviving guards and picked the biggest one, Hank, who seemed smart and had gun sense. Cain trusted Hank; now Fargo was going to trust the big man with Cain's life.

"Hank, can you get him back to Placerville on your own if Cain's on your horse?"

Hank glanced at his boss and nodded. "I can get him there in just over an hour."

Fargo just hoped Cain would live that long.

"Good. Don't take him to the mine. We need the

Brants, who are the people behind all this, to think Cain has been killed.''

"That was Daniel with them as well," Hank said, shaking his head. "Makes no damn sense."

Fargo didn't disagree. "Take Cain to the back door of the Wallace Hotel and ask for Anne. Tell her I told you to put Cain in my room and swear her to secrecy. Then get the doc to fix him up and swear the doc to secrecy as well. Then, if Cain makes it through, be darned sure he stays in that room until I get back there, even if you have to tie him to the bed. Guard him with your life. Understand?''

"Got it," Hank said.

Fargo and the other three men turned back to work on Cain to get him ready to travel.

"Get that shirt off him, and his hat. Switch them with another man's.''

They quickly followed his instructions. Cain moaned slightly as they boosted him up on Hank's horse and tied him in sitting up behind Hank, making sure that his wounds weren't bleeding badly. Both of Cain's legs were roped to the saddle, and he had a rope tied around his stomach holding him tight against Hank. With a hat pulled down low over his face, no one would recognize him.

Cain moaned again as Hank started back up the road toward Placerville. Moaning was a good sign as far as Fargo was concerned. He didn't want to think of what would happen if his good friend died.

Fargo then turned to the other two men, one of which was the big muscled kid named Walt. "Round up the horses and get these bodies to the morgue in Sacramento. Then report to Marshal Davis about what happened. Tell him I'll be contacting him shortly. If he asks, or anyone asks, no matter who it is, Cain is dead. Understand?''

Both men nodded.

"Find a place to lay low and tell the marshal where you'll be. Tell no one what happened. Don't leave until I find you." He handed both of them enough money to cover their rooms and a few drinks and meals, and again they both nodded.

With that, Fargo climbed up on his horse, ignoring the pain in his shoulder.

"Where are you headed?" Walt asked. "You need to get that shoulder looked at."

The kid was right. At some point he was going to have to get his shoulder looked at and cleaned up. He'd do that in Sacramento.

"Right now I have a wagon to follow and a debt to settle. Just do as I ask and I'll find you in Sacramento."

With that, he turned and headed his horse down the trail after the wagon.

Fargo tracked the wagon down the road to within one mile of Sacramento. The three remaining robbers on horseback, including Daniel, seemed to be riding along beside or behind the wagon.

Fargo felt weaker with every passing mile and passing hour, and he could feel that his wound was bleeding again. He was going to need a doctor a lot sooner than he had thought.

The wagon trail branched and the wagon left the main road and headed south on a rarely used road that eventually led back up into the hills. One rider didn't join the wagon, but instead headed into the city spread out below the ridge.

Fargo stared down the road, then at the city below him. It was getting toward dusk and the lights of the city were starting to come on as people lit up the lamps. He could hear the faint sounds of the saloons echoing over the water of the river.

Fargo sat at the intersection in the trail, studying the tracks. He was running out of light, and unless it rained, he could track that wagon tomorrow just fine. And more than likely there was some hideout up in the hills that the bushwhackers called their camp. He would settle the score with them tomorrow, after he was patched up some.

And he would find Daniel and ask him why he had done what he did. Why attack his own father, and maybe even kill him?

Fargo turned the Ovaro toward Sacramento, and within an hour, after making sure his horse was fed and taken care of, he was in the doctor's office hearing the exact things every other doctor had told him over the years.

He was lucky to be alive.

He knew that.

If the lead had hit a little farther in one direction or another, it could have killed him.

He knew that as well.

He needed to rest.

He definitely knew that. Every bone and muscle in his body was shouting that at him.

Fargo just hoped the doctor in Placerville was telling Cain the same thing.

4

Fargo found a cheap hotel off to one side of town. He didn't want to go back to where he and Cain had stayed last time. He needed to hide and to rest. He didn't want Sarah Brant or anyone else to know he had survived just yet.

He barely remembered dropping on the bed and the next thing he knew the sun was burning through his eyelids. The town outside the window was slowly coming alive with the sounds of morning activity.

He eased himself up out of bed, wincing at the pain. It felt as if a cattle stampede had run over his body. He checked the wound on his shoulder where the bullet had gone in and then used a mirror to check the wound on his back where the bullet had left him. Neither wound had bled through the bandages, so for the moment he didn't need to go back to the doctor.

He carefully moved his left shoulder around, feeling for any restriction in movement. Other than the pain from pulling on the wounds, it seemed that the doctor had been right and he had been lucky. The bullet hadn't ripped any muscle or smashed any bone. It had just gone through him. In a week he wouldn't even notice it much, besides the two new scars.

What he wished he could do was head back to Placerville, see if his good friend had survived, and let Anne tend to him in that big, soft feather bed of hers.

But that would come soon enough. Right now he had a score to settle. And he had to find Daniel.

He eased on a clean shirt that didn't have blood

and bullet holes, then buckled his Colt back to his hip and headed out. After a quick stop to check on the Ovaro, he headed for Marshal Davis's office, keeping his hat down low over his eyes to try to avoid anyone recognizing him. At least one of the bushwhackers was in town somewhere and for the moment he wanted them thinking he might be dead, along with Cain. It would make them bolder and more careless in whatever play they were making for Cain's mine.

The marshal actually seemed glad to see him, and a little worried. "You all right? One of Cain's men said you were wounded."

"Took one in the shoulder," Fargo said, "but I've had worse."

Marshal Davis nodded. "Sorry to hear about Cain. He was a good man."

Fargo glanced around to make sure no one was in the jail who could overhear the conversation. He trusted his sense about this man, and he knew this marshal's reputation. The man could be trusted.

"Cain was shot, but he may not be dead just yet," Fargo said. "I don't honestly know. I sent him with one of his men to hide in a hotel in Placerville. I don't know if he made it or not, but I figured it was the better hand to play, letting the bushwhackers think he was dead."

The marshal looked confused. "Why?"

Fargo spent the next few minutes telling the marshal everything he knew about Henry and Sarah Brant, and all the details, including Daniel's presence among the robbers.

"The kid's using the neighbor's mine to make a play on his father," the marshal said, clearly disgusted.

"Maybe, maybe not," Fargo said. "Before he joined in with the Brants, Daniel was a good kid. A little gold hungry, but still a good kid. I think Sarah Brant is the one pulling his strings."

"Henry Brant is known for cutting corners and taking shortcuts. And I've heard his mine is starting to play out. It would make sense he's using the kid."

"I heard the same thing about the mine," Fargo said. "And there are rumors that they're digging underground toward Cain's tunnels. But to confirm all that, I have to find Daniel."

"If he's still alive," Marshal Davis said. "If Henry Brant thinks that Cain is dead, it would be simple to kill Daniel and take over the Cain mine."

"My thinking exactly," Fargo said. That was his biggest worry outside of Cain living. Daniel didn't have a very long life ahead of him if Fargo didn't get this cleared up.

"So what can I do to help?" Marshal Davis asked.

Fargo had been hoping the marshal would ask that question. "I've got some ore to recover, so I could really use your help looking through town for Daniel, if you know what he looks like."

"I've met him. You think he's here?"

"I'm not sure, but one of the robbers left the wagon and came into town. I'm guessing it was Daniel. If I don't find him with the gold, he's either here or already dead."

"What do you want us to do with him if we find him?"

"Don't arrest him," Fargo said. "That would tip them off to what you know. Just keep an eye on him until I get back and can work some truth out of the kid."

"You got it," the marshal said. Then he smiled. "Your men are down at the Mine Shaft Saloon near the river. You need a few more men to go with you on your recovery operation? I could spare a few to join you. I wouldn't mind coming along myself, to be honest."

Fargo shook his head. "No, thanks. This one is personal. I'm going to go it alone. I'll let you know what happens."

"Can't say as I blame you, Fargo," the marshal said. "Good hunting."

Two hours later, after a good breakfast, Fargo

turned south at the intersection off the Placerville road, once again following the wagon tracks.

Three miles south of Sacramento, the tracks turned off the main trail and headed back east and into a deep valley coming down out of the mountains. There was no doubt that this trail dead-ended up this valley. The trail had obviously been seldom used, so it would have almost no traffic. Fargo had to respect the choice of a hideout by the robbers. It was close enough to town and the Placerville road, yet isolated and easy to defend and guard.

Fargo veered off the trail and took the Ovaro up a ridge, moving slowly and carefully, following game trails that ran along the valley sides.

An hour later he found what he was looking for. Near where the canyon turned into a box canyon against three steep walls of rocks, a wisp of smoke from a fire drifted above the trees.

From that camp there was only one way out. It was a camp that was easy to defend from attack, but it also made Fargo's job a lot easier. He had them trapped like rats in a water barrel.

He left his horse in a safe place, then with his heavy carbine in hand, he scouted the area around the camp.

There looked to be three men in the camp. Daniel was not one of the men. Fargo had been right that it had been Daniel who had gone into Sacramento. Fargo just hoped the marshal and his men could find him and protect the stupid kid.

At the moment the men were standing around the campfire, drinking coffee. Cain's wagon sat near where they had tied the horses, and it was still loaded with the gold. Clearly, this was just a stopover point until someone told them what to do with their loot.

They realized too late that they'd been joined by a fierce-looking man with a Henry and a real unfriendly voice.

One of the men started to go for his gun but his friend said, "Don't be stupid, Dave."

"I want the guns pitched as far as you can throw 'em. Then I want your boots off and I want you to toss them too. Far as they'll go."

"Who the hell are you?"

"Nobody important. But you killed somebody important, at least to me. So just be thankful I don't shoot you bastards down right here and now."

The harsh words made them move quicker. They bitched and moaned of course—it was humiliating, throwing away your guns and boots—but they did it.

When that was done, Fargo said, "Now hitch up the horses. I'm taking the wagon."

"They'll think we took it," one of them complained.

"I'd say that's your problem, not mine. Now get it done."

A mile beyond where the men had camped, Fargo found a place to pull the wagon off into some cover behind some rocks so it couldn't be seen from the trail. He tied up the horses and then went back for his own horse.

He tied the Ovaro to the rear of the wagon. When he got back to the main trail, instead of turning back north, he went south away from Sacramento. It would be a good ten miles out of the way to circle around and back into town that way, but that was better than taking a chance of meeting any of the Brant men coming for the gold.

Right now it was better to let Brant and his people think that his men had been robbed of the ore they had robbed from Cain. It might give Daniel another day of life.

Maybe.

He got the gold into the bank before it closed and then told Marshal Davis where he could find the robbers. So far, the marshal had had no luck finding Daniel, but as he said, most of his men didn't know what Cain's son looked like.

"We'll find him," Fargo said. He thanked the marshal and then headed to where Cain's two men should be waiting for him.

He found them both sitting in the Mine Shaft Saloon at a corner table, their backs to the wall. They both had drinks in front of them, but it was clear they were too worried to drink much. A deck of cards lay on the table between them, but no cards were dealt.

One was a solid middle-aged man with a wide mustache. His name was Jim. The other was Walt. From this angle, he looked like he could bend a railroad spike with his bare hands. Cain had told Fargo that both men were good in a fight and both had ridden the range at times. Fargo had a good feeling about them.

As Fargo entered the run-down saloon, both had their hats pulled low over their eyes. But when they recognized him, they jumped up and pushed their hats back, smiling. Patience and waiting were clearly not their strong suits.

"How ya doin'?" Jim asked as Fargo approached the table.

"Are we going after them?" Walt asked.

"Doing fine," Fargo said, indicating that the men should follow him out to the street. "Doctor said I would live. And I already took care of the robbers and Cain's gold is delivered and where it belongs."

"Fargo, the stories they tell about you don't go anywhere near far enough," Jim said, shaking his head.

Fargo didn't want to ask just what tales Jim had heard.

"Damn," Walt said. "We missed all the fun."

"I have a feeling the fun is just beginning," Fargo said. "If you call men getting shot *fun*."

"If the man deserves to be shot, yeah I do," Walt said.

Fargo glanced at the strong kid and said nothing.

"Any news about Cain?" Jim asked.

"Nothing," Fargo said. "We'll find out soon enough. Right now we have to find Daniel."

"He was part of the bunch that robbed us and shot

his father," Walt said, his words showing his disgust and anger. "I couldn't believe it, but he was. I had a clear shot at him and didn't take it. Wish I had now."

"I had a clear shot as well," Fargo said. "Daniel may have had reasons for what he did, or maybe he was duped by Sarah Brant. We have to find him and find out. He's in town somewhere. Or at least he was yesterday."

"I've heard stories about that Brant woman," Jim said as they reached the sidewalk and Fargo led them toward the center of town. "They say her mother left because of her."

"I was warned to stay out of her clutches because she liked to cut off men's privates," Walt said, shuddering. "But everyone says she's a looker."

"I met her once," Fargo said. "And I don't doubt either story. And if Daniel was wrapped up in her charms, there's no telling what he would have done for her. But right now we've got to find him."

"Mind if I pound some sense into him if I find him?" Jim asked.

"Yes, I do mind," Fargo said. "You find him, either of you, and you come and get me. My gut tells me this kid is in danger. We have to find him before they do, now that they think his father is dead."

"I sure hope he's not," Walt said.

Fargo couldn't do anything but agree with that. He wasn't letting himself think about Cain dying.

When Fargo reached a general store close to the center of town, he told Walt to go south along Main, checking out every hotel and saloon. "Ask the desk clerks if Daniel Parker has checked in."

Fargo sent Jim north doing the same thing.

"I'm going to check some of the brothels," Fargo said.

"You get all the good jobs," Walt said, smiling.

"Just had more experience in those places," Fargo said. "We meet right back here in an hour. And remember, don't let him see you if you can help it. Just come and find me. Don't do anything to spook him."

Both men nodded. Fargo left first. Before Walt and Jim separated, Walt said, "Not everybody's gonna believe us."

"Believe us about what?" Jim said.

"Working with Fargo. The Trailsman."

Jim laughed. "You're probably right. I met a newspaperman once—he told me he didn't think that Fargo even existed."

"I'll bet some of it's exaggerated, though," Walt said.

"Some is. But not by Fargo. People just like to have heroes and they make up things about them."

"One thing I heard was that he fought two black bears at a time."

Jim laughed. "I'm pretty sure that didn't happen."

"Another thing I heard was that down in Louisiana he killed an alligator with his bare hands."

"Now that one I know is true. Met a man who actually saw it."

"But he ain't—I mean, he could still be killed."

"Sure he could. Just like us."

"He's prob'ly been up against tougher men than Brant before."

"Tougher, maybe. But not any greedier."

Walt nodded agreement and the men went on their separate ways.

After three times out and back, none of them had had any luck, so Fargo bought them all lavish steak-and-potato dinners. If Cain lived, he wouldn't mind feeding the men who were trying to save his son. And if he didn't live, he wouldn't care that Fargo had spent his money.

In the three hours, Fargo had personally visited more than a dozen brothels, been propositioned by a dozen women, and been tossed out of one house by a madam who knew him from Denver. He had helped one of her girls get away from her to marry a grocer who was headed west. It seemed the madam still held a grudge and could handle a very large Colt.

Both Walt and Jim complained about their feet hurting and how they hadn't realized just how big Sacramento had become. Fargo was surprised at that as well. He'd always thought of Sacramento as a bustling but fairly small city.

After dinner they headed back out.

Two hours later Fargo found Daniel sitting in the front parlor of a brothel. He was drunk, so drunk that he could hardly move. It was clear he had been flashing money around like he had more than enough of it. And Daniel's money was like honey to the girls, who took turns sitting on his lap, kissing him, giving him more drinks, and relieving him of his money.

Fargo walked into the parlor and pushed one girl gently aside before yanking Daniel to his feet. "You're coming with me, kid."

"Hey," protested the madam, a large woman with enormous breasts that seemed to want to escape from her low-cut sheer robe in a thousand different directions. "You can't go taking my customers."

"Yeah," Daniel said, trying to pull away from Fargo's grasp. "Who are you anyway?"

"I work for your father," Fargo said, then solidly punched Daniel square in the nose, sending blood gushing and the kid slumping, out cold. More than likely he hit the kid a little harder than he needed to, but he was still damn angry at Daniel.

Fargo held Daniel up and fished for the kid's money, tossing the entire wad of bills to the madam. "Sorry for the mess and the problem," Fargo said. "The kid's now broke."

"Pleasure doing business with you," the madam said as the bills vanished into the massive canyon that was her cleavage.

Fargo tossed Daniel up over his good shoulder and went out the door held open by one of the girls, ignoring the looks from passersby as he headed back to where he was to meet Jim and Walt.

He propped Daniel up on a bench and wiped some of the blood from his face while he waited. The kid was still out cold and likely would be until he slept off all the booze.

Fargo sat down beside the kid, watching everyone on the street. It had been a long day and the wounds in his shoulder were aching again. He could use a good night's sleep as well.

When Walt and Jim finally arrived, Fargo had Walt carry Daniel back to the Mine Shaft Saloon. The hotel attached to the saloon was where they had stayed and left their gear, expecting to return tonight. They put Daniel on the floor in their room and tied him securely to the large metal-framed bed.

Fargo got his own room, then went back to see if the kid was awake yet. It was no surprise that he wasn't.

"Take turns guarding him. And make sure he doesn't get away. He's got a lot of talking to do tomorrow. I'm in the room next door."

For the second night, the moment Fargo lay down on the bed he was out like someone had snuffed a candle. The rays of the sun the next morning woke him.

This morning his shoulder felt a little better. He checked under one bandage and then pulled it off. The doc had stitched both wounds and they looked like they were healing just fine. He started to put on his shirt when he realized the heavy stitches would catch on the cloth. He quickly taped the bandage back on. Maybe a couple more days and he could again wear a shirt without it. Maybe.

The room next door sounded like a factory going full tilt. All three men were snoring like it was a competition to see who could be the loudest. And to be honest, Fargo couldn't tell.

Walt was in the chair, his pistol on his lap. Jim was on the bed, and Daniel was still tied up on the floor.

Fargo moved silently just inside the door and then slammed it behind him.

Walt came out of the chair, sending his gun spinning across the floor.

Jim jerked and rolled off the bed on the window side, coming up a moment later with his gun in his hand.

Daniel jerked upward and then was slammed back against the floor by the ropes holding him.

Fargo forced himself not to smile. "Good morning. I hope everyone slept well. I know I did."

Rubbing the sleep from his eyes, Walt sheepishly moved to get his gun and Jim stood up, holstering his.

"Oh, my head hurts," Daniel said, moaning. "And my nose. You broke my nose. And if someone doesn't find me a bedpan or an outhouse real soon, there's going to be a mess right here on the floor." Then he looked at Fargo with sober recognition. "Now I recognize you from last night. You're Fargo."

"Untie him," Fargo said, "and we'll all take him out back just to make sure one of us stays awake."

As Walt leaned over to untie him, Daniel recognized him too. Then he glanced over and recognized Jim. The kid who had been trying to show a strong face against the hangover and likely kidnappers suddenly broke down and cried like a girl.

"I didn't know, I didn't know," he kept saying through the sobs.

Walt finished with the ropes and stepped back, glancing around at Fargo with a puzzled look on his face.

"Get him on his feet and out back," Fargo said to both Jim and Walt.

They yanked up the sobbing man like he was a rag doll and half carried him out the door and down the hall toward the outhouse.

"What didn't you know?" Fargo asked Daniel as they went through the back door. The alley was a small street lined down the center with a dozen outhouses serving the hotels on each side. No one else was in the alley at the moment, but there was no way of telling if there was someone in one of the narrow, wooden structures.

"That it was my father's gold they were after," Dan-

62

iel sobbed, tears flowing over his broken nose and making lines in the dried blood on his face. "I didn't know. Sarah said it was from the Constitution mine. I'm pretty sure her father's behind all this."

"And that allows you to rob and kill men for gold?" Fargo asked, even more disgusted now at the sobbing boy. No wonder Sarah Brant could manipulate this kid. He was as weak and as stupid as they came.

Walt opened the outhouse door and Fargo shoved the kid inside really hard, slamming him into the back wood wall.

"Come out when you're finished and can stand on your own two feet and be a man."

Fargo looked first at Jim, then at Walt. "Both of you stay here and guard him. And if he tries to escape, shoot him."

"Gladly," Walt said.

Jim only nodded, but clearly didn't disagree with Walt.

"When he's finished, take him back to the room and tie him up again. I'll be back."

With that, Fargo strode off toward Marshal Davis's office. He was so disgusted at the son of his good friend, he didn't know what to do.

Fargo stamped up onto a wooden sidewalk and brushed past two men. He needed to calm down and think straight. And the best way to do that was to talk to the marshal and find out if he had any more information about the men in that box canyon yesterday.

He knew it was Sarah Brant and her father behind all this. Daniel had told him that much.

"Fargo, you sure made a lot of enemies up there when you made those men throw away their boots and guns," the marshal laughed as Fargo entered the office.

"Just doing my civic duty, Marshal," Fargo said. "You station a couple of men up there to watch for who comes up that trail?"

The marshal smiled real big. "Actually, didn't need

to. They arrived while we were still there. Two men, both foremen at the Brant mine, rode right into our trap just easy as could be."

"Are they talking?"

"Nope, not yet. They're claiming they were just on the wrong trail and lost. We're going to hold them until the circuit court rides through here next week. I figured I might as well let a judge decide what to do with them and keep them out of the coming fight."

Fargo nodded. This man was not stupid. He had been in the West as long as Fargo had and knew what a battle between two major mines was like. "Thanks. I appreciate that."

"So, you find Daniel?"

"Yup," Fargo said, the anger at the kid coming back. "In a brothel, drunk as a skunk. We sobered him up and he started crying like a little girl, claiming he didn't know it was his father's wagon full of gold."

"What, he thought he was out riding for fun or something?"

"Claimed he thought they were after the Constitution's gold. Claimed that Sarah Brant had told him that."

"Robbing and killing for a woman," Marshal Davis said, shaking his head in disgust. "There's nothing new under the sun, is there?"

"Doesn't seem like it," Fargo said.

"So, you want to bring him in and let him cry here in jail and point some fingers? It might save a fight up in Placerville."

"I honestly don't know what I want to do with the kid," Fargo said. "I feel like I owe my friend Cain to take care of his son and get him back to his father. But Cain may just turn him over to you anyway. If Cain is still alive, he's going to be as disgusted as I am. This kid was involved in robbing his own father's gold and killing his men. I can't imagine Cain allowing that to stand and be forgotten."

"Knowing Cain, I can't either," Marshal Davis said. "But to be honest, if Cain is dead, I'd want to take

Daniel up into the hills and put a bunch of bullets in his arms and legs while he tries to crawl away."

Fargo looked at the marshal and then laughed. "I knew I liked you for a reason, Marshal."

They both laughed. Then the marshal said, "Well, let me know what you do with him. But keep in mind that this area has tamed down enough that there is real law here these days that sometimes gets the job done."

Fargo stuck out his hand and shook the marshal's firm grip. "Just as long as we get justice, that's all I care about."

As Fargo opened the door, the sound of gunfire broke over the city from the direction of Fargo's hotel. His gut told him that it had to do with Daniel.

He glanced back at the marshal, then took off at a run, the marshal after a moment pounding along right beside him, matching him stride for stride. Both of them had guns out of leather and both were ready to fight.

The gunfire lasted for less than twenty seconds and then there was silence before the normal sounds of the city filled back in. Fargo didn't like the sound of that silence at all.

As he and the marshal rounded the corner to get behind the hotel, he saw Walt step from behind a large wooden container and stare at the outhouse, his gun still in his hand. A moment later, Jim came out the back door of the hotel, looking around cautiously, his gun still in his hand as well.

"What happened?" Fargo demanded as he got close.

Jim pointed at the open second-story window in the back of the hotel across the narrow street filled with outhouses. And Walt pointed to the roofline of another building.

"They started firing before we had time to react," Jim said. "There were four, maybe five of them. They had us in a cross fire."

"Five," Walt said. "We took cover and returned

fire, but they didn't seem to care about us. They just poured lead into the outhouse and then backed away as we fired back."

"They were firing rifles," Jim said. "Some of the shots were going clear through the outhouse and pounding into the dirt."

Fargo didn't want to open the bullet-riddled wooden outhouse, but he forced himself to.

Inside, Daniel had been sitting with his britches still up and his belt tied. His eyes were wide-open in surprise and red from crying. His shirt and pants were a mass of blood and holes. A moment after Fargo opened the door, Daniel fell forward into the dirt.

"There was nothing we could do," Walt said.

"Yeah," Jim said. "The kid just sat in there and cried and wouldn't come out, right up to the moment they opened fire."

The marshal spun around to a deputy who had just run up. "Get men guarding all the ways out of town. Look for a group of five men leaving on horseback."

Fargo shook his head. "No use, Marshal. Those men are long gone. We'll have to take care of them later."

Fargo felt sorry all over again for his old friend Cain. If the man was still alive, he'd now have to hear that his son had been murdered.

5

Two hours later, they had Daniel's body wrapped in a tarp and strapped on the back of a horse as they headed out of Sacramento. Fargo scouted ahead of the other two, making sure that no one would attack them on the way back. He didn't think anyone would, but he liked being prepared. And with the Brant thugs, there was no telling what they would do next. Besides, scouting helped keep his mind off of the coming task of telling Cain that his son was dead. More than likely Cain had seen Daniel during the robbery, so it was impossible to guess how Cain would react to his death.

If Cain was still alive.

Fargo wouldn't let himself think too long about the possibility that Cain hadn't made it. The man had been so strong through so many fights. He had to be here for this one. Sarah and Henry Brant were going to pay for what they had done. Fargo was going to see to that. And their men were going to pay as well. They couldn't be allowed to take over Cain's mine, whether Cain and Daniel were alive or not.

At the intersection in the road that led either into town or to Cain's mine, Fargo left Walt and Jim to the task of taking Daniel's body back to the Cain home. He kept on going into town, got his Ovaro stabled and brushed and fed, and finally headed to the hotel. He couldn't delay it any longer. He had to face the outcome of this eventually. At least he was going to see Anne again.

The bright sun of the day beat down on him as he walked, heating his shirt and making his shoulder ache.

Fargo went through the door into the saloon and, like the first time, Anne was behind the bar. He couldn't believe how much just seeing her cheered him.

She happened to glance up as he let the batwings close behind him. Her face lit up like a child seeing a Christmas present.

She rushed around the bar and hugged him so hard, his wounds hurt. But he didn't care. Just having her against him, pressing into him again, felt great.

She took him by the hand and led him into the back room, to her private office.

"Are you all right?" she asked. "I heard you were shot."

"Through the shoulder," Fargo said. He pointed to the wound on the front. "It came out the back. I'm going to be just fine. But tell me, how's Cain?"

The smile dropped from her face and she motioned for him to sit down in a chair near her desk where she could sit and face him. "He didn't make it through the first night. I'm so sorry, Skye. The doc did everything he could, but the wound was just too bad."

Fargo felt himself go numb.

His friend had asked for his help, his protection, and now both his friend and his friend's son were dead.

Fargo stared at the wall above Anne. How could he have miscalculated so badly? How could he have let the Brants get so far ahead of him?

Anne sat there, holding his hand, letting him take in the news, the very thing he hadn't let himself think about over the last few days.

Finally, she said softly, "Tell me what happened."

He went back over the details of the last three days, from the ambush to the killing of Daniel.

"What's going to happen to Cain's mine and all his gold and buildings?" she asked after a moment.

"I don't know the answer to that," Fargo said. "But I can tell you this: Brant and his men will not get it. Not while I'm alive."

She reached forward and squeezed his hand, smiling. "I know that. But we need to put some sort of legal basis under this and get the mine to someone. Did Cain have a will?"

Fargo shrugged. "I doubt it. Not the type."

"So, who deserves to get that mine and those buildings and all the money in the banks in Sacramento?"

Fargo looked over at her, then smiled as he saw where she was heading. "His men. Some of them have died for him and that mine."

"Exactly," Anne said. "I've heard of a few owners giving parts or all of their mines to their workers. It's possible to do."

Fargo stood and then picked up Anne and held her close to him, kissing her hard. "Get a lawyer and a judge ready. I'll be back with Cain's will."

Anne laughed. "I thought you said he wasn't the type to write up a will."

"I could be wrong," Fargo said.

He kissed her soft lips one more time, enjoying the promise of a night in the feather bed with her, then turned and headed out the door. They first had to secure Cain's mine legally for the men who would defend it; then it would be time for some real frontier justice.

The last miner came up from the mine, wiped off his face, and joined the meeting forming in the large bunkhouse. Men sat, sprawled, and stood everywhere, crowded around the wooden bunks. A number of women from the kitchens had joined the meeting as well.

Fargo couldn't believe how many men and women had depended on Cain and his Sharon's Dream mine.

Two hours before, Fargo had met Hank, Walt, and

Jim at the ranch house. They had put Daniel's body in the root cellar until they could bury it with his father in the small mine cemetery.

All three of them thought that they were now out of a job. They had no doubt that Brant would jump Cain's claim and take over by sheer force. They were pretty much ready to bury Cain and Daniel and head down the trail. None of them would ever work for Brant.

Fargo took less than a minute to describe his idea. It got them excited again, and ready to fight.

"One small problem," Fargo had said. "Can any of you write?"

Jim could. With Hank's help, since he was the chief foreman and had been Cain's right-hand man for the past six months, they got Cain's safe opened and some samples of Cain's writing laid out on the table.

After an hour of practice, Jim started writing the simple will that gave the mine over to Daniel. And then, if Daniel died within a year of Cain, the mine and all its assets were to go in equal shares to every man and woman working for the mine at the time of Daniel's death.

As Jim practiced writing in Cain's handwriting, Hank put together a list of the people who were working for Cain this last week. Fargo wouldn't let him put his name on the list. He had no desire to own part of a mine.

Two hours after they started, the will was finished and the men were gathered.

Fargo stood back as Hank told all the men the bad news of both Cain's and Daniel's deaths.

"The funeral for both of them will be at sunrise tomorrow morning," Hank said. "I expect you all to be there."

There was a long moment of silence as the news sank in. Then Hank cleared his throat and went on. "I hold in my hand Cain's will."

Hank held up the paper and the envelope that had

contained it. "Basically, it gives the mine and all the assets to Daniel."

There was a murmuring among the men, but no one asked the next obvious question out loud.

"However," Hank said, his voice carrying clearly in the crowded bunkhouse. "The will also says that if Daniel dies within a year of Cain, the mine is to go in equal parts to everyone working at Sharon's Dream at the time of Daniel's death. Officially, we now all own this mine and all the gold and assets that come out of it."

The noise suddenly became deafening as the men shouted and cheered and slapped one another on the back.

Hank smiled and let them go on for a moment, then held up his hands for silence. "In one hour, twenty of us, with the help of Fargo here, are going to make sure this will is filed officially in the courthouse. However, we're not out of the woods just yet."

Hank nodded to Fargo and he stepped forward. "There is clear proof that the Brants and their men are behind the deaths of Cain and his son."

Shouts of anger filled the room and Fargo let the anger wash over him. He was going to need all of them angry if they were going to win the coming fight.

Hank held up his hands for the men to calm down and let Fargo go on.

After there was silence again, Fargo continued. "They're going to make a move on this mine, both above- and belowground."

"Over my dead body," one miner shouted, and the others agreed loudly.

"Let's hope it doesn't come to that," Fargo said. "But it looks like we're going to have a war and it's going to start real soon."

"We're ready," one man hollered, and the others shouted their agreement.

"We're all going to have to fight together. You should all wear guns at all times until this is settled and if you don't have a gun, talk to Hank after the meeting and he'll get you set up. And we're going to need the best shots among you posted as sentries along the ridgeline between here and the Brant mine. And others guarding the road and the other sides of this area."

"We're with you, Fargo," a man shouted.

"Good," Fargo said. "Now let's get to work."

6

The Eastern papers often mocked the way justice worked in the West. In the East, black-robed men deliberated over laws and precedent before handing down their decisions. When they spoke to the lawyers before them they tended to sound self-important and pompous. At least that was the way the Western papers liked to depict those Eastern magistrates.

Here, the papers enjoyed judges who occasionally winked at the laws and statutes that supposedly guided them and made decisions quickly and without undue fuss.

This was generally the way it worked, anyway. But Fargo wondered if he wasn't dealing with a transplanted Easterner when he met Judge Rupert T. D. Hodges, who was to rule on the filing of Cain's will.

Peering over the gold-rimmed glasses that had slid down his pointed nose, Hodges constantly rubbed his fingers against a bald pate and sniffed as if he was coming down with a cold. He sat in a room that rivaled a small library in number of books. In addition to a massive globe, an equally massive lantern, and a relatively modest pipe rack, the hardwood floor shone and the mullioned windows gleamed with daylight.

Fargo was used to hanging judges who swilled whiskey and befouled the room with the smoke of cheap cigars as they made their rash and often mistaken rulings.

Fargo had told the judge why the people named on the list he handed over should become the official owners in equal parts of the mine. The judge offered neither word nor even expression. He lowered his head and began his seemingly endless consideration of the appeal.

Fargo and Walt and Jim exchanged many useless glances as they stood before his desk. Once, Jim sighed deeply. The judge peered up over his glasses and frowned. "Are you in a hurry, young man?"

It was like being back in a schoolhouse when the teacher decided to pick on you and make your life hell. "No, sir," Jim said, his face red.

"Good. Because I'm not either."

A well-polished grandfather clock in one corner ticked off the long minutes. The judge had a law book open on the right side of his desk. He consulted it frequently.

Then came the surprise. The judge looked up and said, "I'm granting your request. The people on your list will become equal owners of the mine." He pushed his glasses up on his nose and called for his court clerk to come into the office. He spent a minute having his clerk read the will and the list of names into the court record, then said simply: "Good day, gentlemen."

Outside the county courthouse, Fargo stood with Hank, Walt, and Jim. The sun had gone behind the mountains, casting the valley and the town into shadows. It was still hot, but there was the promise of a cool evening in the air.

"That judge was a right friendly gent," Jim said. "Figured he'd invite us all for a drink."

"Yeah." Walt laughed. "With poison in it."

Fargo laughed too, but then got right back to work.

"Get everyone ready and guards posted," Fargo said to them. "When Brant and his daughter hear about this, they may try a full-out attack on the mine. If they can blow up the mine opening or shut you down in some way, then they can tunnel into the vein and claim it as theirs. Be ready. Both aboveground and below. For the first time, we're ahead of them, and they're not going to like that."

"Let them come," Hank said. "Thanks to your idea, every man working the mine has a real reason to fight. I doubt Brant's men do. And that's going to make a difference."

"I have no doubt about that," Fargo said.

"What are you going to do?" Walt asked.

"Get a good night's sleep, first off," Fargo said, smiling. "Don't worry—I'll be around. I'm going to be like a kid with a stick poking at a beehive when it comes to Brant. I have a score to settle."

"If you need any help, you know where we'll be," Hank said. "And as long as you're here helping us, we'll keep paying you the same price Cain was paying you."

"No need," Fargo said. "Save your money. You have to split it a lot of ways. And besides, I tend to work alone. But thanks."

"Thank you," Hank said. He shook Fargo's hand and then the three of them headed back to their mine.

Fargo turned and headed for the Wallace Hotel. Anne had gone back ahead of him after the judge had declared the will official. This time he went in the hotel entrance, nodding at the desk clerk before climbing the stairs to his room. Before he could put the key in the door, a soft voice came from down the hall.

"Where do you think you're going, mister?" Anne poked her head out her door and smiled at him.

"I was hoping to get cleaned up, then a little dinner with a beautiful woman, a short love-making session, and a long night's sleep. Do you know anyone who might want to help me with all that?"

Anne laughed. "I sure do. This way." She stuck her arm out the door and gestured that he should come to her.

She swung open the door as he neared, showing him that she was standing there completely naked.

The sight took his breath away. She was one of the most beautiful women he had ever known.

He stopped for a moment just to stare, then stepped inside, afraid to even try a comment.

She pointed to the large tub in the corner. "I just happened to be getting ready for a bath and figured you might want to join me."

"I could use a bath, but you probably hadn't noticed," he said.

She laughed. "Now that you mention it—" She looked into his lake blue eyes for a moment, then kissed him solidly on the lips.

He wrapped his arms around her shoulders and pulled her close, feeling her breasts push into him. It felt really good being back here with her.

She pushed him away and then slowly worked to take off his shirt. When she saw his bandages, she gasped.

"Are you sure you're all right?"

"Let's check," he said. "I could use your help trimming some of the stitches the doc used on me."

Carefully, with her help, he pulled off the bandage on his shoulder. Under it, the hole where the bullet had gone in looked red, but not swollen with any infection. It looked like the doctor had done a good job on that one.

She turned him around and carefully pulled off the bandage in back. That hole was slightly larger from what the doc had told him. Exit wounds usually were.

"How's it look?" he asked her.

"Painful," she said. "But healing. Trimming the ends of the stitching won't hurt you, and a bath might even help them a little, make sure they're clean. Do you have a fresh shirt to wear?"

"One," he said.

"We'll send the rest of your things to the laundry tomorrow. You need to keep clean shirts on these wounds until they finish healing."

"Thank you, nurse," he said, turning around and kissing her. "Anyone ever tell you that you have a great bedside manner?"

"And I thought it was just the uniform," she said.

He laughed. "That helps, I have to admit."

She helped him out of his boots and trousers, then into the tub.

It took him a moment to settle in to the hot water, but once he was in, he could feel the aches and tiredness in his muscles slowly draining away. There was sure something to be said about hot baths. At least after a few days like he had just had.

She scrubbed him down with a rough sponge like he was a horse, being careful around his wounds and then using only her soft hands on his private parts.

He tried to wash her as well, especially those hidden areas between her legs, but she kept moving his hands away, telling him to wait his turn.

Finally, when she was done scrubbing off a layer of his skin, she told him to lie back and enjoy the moment.

She moved to the other end of the large, narrow tub and sat up on the end, her feet still touching his, her legs open so that he could see her most intimate parts. If this wasn't heaven, he didn't know what could beat it.

Slowly, not missing an inch, she used the sponge to wash herself. She started with her neck, then worked down her arms, bending down every so often to dip the sponge in the water.

He watched her breasts move as she moved. He watched the soapy water run down her body, over her breasts, down her stomach, and through the fine brown hair between her legs. He was mesmerized following the water, staring at her every movement.

He was as hard as he ever remembered being, and it took every ounce of willpower he had not to take her right then.

She seemed to spend extra time on her breasts, moving them around, soaping them again, rubbing them.

Never, in all his life, had he felt so aroused by simply watching a woman. He never wanted the moment to end.

She had the look of intense lust that he had come to recognize. Her eyes were slits, not really seeing anything, her face filled with a smile of contentment.

She let out a low moan and looked at him.

He reached for her and she slipped down into the water, moving quickly to impale herself on his thick rod. As her warm slickness settled over him, she sighed and then shuddered, reaching a peak all on her own, without him even having to move.

He held her for a moment as her shuddering eased. Then he started moving under her, sloshing the water slowly back and forth in long, rolling waves.

She joined in his movements perfectly, holding him while being careful to not touch his wounds.

Faster and faster they went, the waves on the water becoming like those on an angry lake in a violent storm.

After a moment, Fargo knew he couldn't hold on any longer and he pushed up into her, emptying himself as she again reached another peak and shuddered with him.

They lay there, she in his arms, he still inside her, letting the waves calm.

All he could think about was how good this felt. How good she felt.

Finally, as he softened and started to slip out of her, she looked up at him and smiled, her green eyes alive and glowing. "You sure know how to make a girl hungry. I think the chef has a couple of special steaks in the kitchen cut just for us."

He laughed and kissed her. "Woman, I think that fits in to my evening plans perfectly."

She was right. The steaks were perfect, thick and juicy. And the conversation was even better. Not one word about Sarah or Henry Brant or Cain or Daniel.

They made love again slowly in her feather bed after dinner and the next thing he knew, the sun was coming up again and she was gone. How she managed to get up, get dressed, and leave without waking him was beyond his imagination. Yet somehow she had managed it.

In his own room, he put on his last clean shirt, gently pulling it over his now exposed wounds. Then he left the rest of his clothes in a pile on his bed for Anne's laundry service to take and clean. After getting shot, he needed a new shirt as well.

With his Colt tied to his hip, he went looking for Anne. He found her happily doing paperwork in her office.

"Morning," she said. "I was just about to wake you to join me for breakfast."

"Timing is everything," he said. "You missed the chance to see me without my britches on again."

Her eyes twinkled and she smiled slyly. "Oh, I took a look before I left."

He opened his mouth to say something back and found nothing to say as the image of her standing over him looking at his manhood flashed through his mind.

She laughed and came around the desk, taking him by the arm and escorting him to the dining room.

Over breakfast, the conversation turned to what they had both avoided the night before. And he started it.

"You know, being seen with me could be dangerous for you."

She nodded. "I know that. It's a chance I'm willing to take."

"But I'm not," he said.

She frowned. "I don't like the sound of that, Fargo."

"I was wondering if you would do me a very big favor."

"I'm listening," she said, but not agreeing to anything yet.

"I ruined a shirt with two bullet holes. It was a favorite shirt of mine."

"I can imagine it was," she said, looking puzzled.

"If I escorted you to the train station in Sacramento, would you be so kind as to go into San Francisco for a few days, maybe a week, to find me a new one? It was a very special shirt."

She laughed and leaned forward and kissed him. "Why would you think I would do that? I'm not really into running away from a fight, you know."

"I know that about you," he said. "It's one of the many things I admire about you more than I can tell you. However, look around."

He swept his arm around at the beautiful dining room and hotel before she could say anything. "You have an investment and people here to protect. Reg, for one. Just being known to be close to me will put you and them in danger, especially with what I plan on doing very shortly."

He took her hands in his across the tablecloth as she stared into his eyes. "I've lost one friend this week to these people. I can't imagine losing you as well, and if you stay here, I'll be more worried about protecting you than doing what I need to do."

She stared at him for the longest time, never letting her gaze waver from his eyes. Finally, she said softly, "What color?"

It was his turn now to look puzzled.

"If you're sending me all the way to San Francisco to shop for a shirt for you, I should at least know what color you want."

7

An hour later, he and Anne were headed down the road. For the first time since he had seen her in Colorado, she had her riding clothes on. She looked just as good in them as she did in a dress. Maybe better, if that was possible. And she was an expert on a horse, riding smoothly with the animal's motions, clearly comfortable. There wasn't much about this woman that Fargo didn't like. In fact, he couldn't think of one thing.

Since no one knew she was leaving with him except Reg, and she had told him just a few minutes before she left, Fargo wasn't too worried about being attacked on their ride. He let himself enjoy it, while at the same time keeping an eye out ahead for any problems.

Along the way, they talked about various things. She outlined a few problems in the hotel business in general, and her fear that Placerville was about to take a turn for the worse. He told her of some of the troubles at Sharon's Dream. It was a good conversation with a beautiful companion on a clear, warm day. He wished it could have gone on longer, but in what seemed like no time, they had her horse stabled and were at the station, standing in front of the train that was about to depart for San Francisco. She'd earlier stopped and changed into a dress.

"I'll wire you at the hotel in San Francisco when this thing is over and meet you here when you come back."

She nodded. "Just be careful."

"I always am," he said. "Thanks for doing this for me."

"It's a lot to go through for one shirt," she said, smiling up at him. Then she kissed him full on the lips, pulling him down against her. After a moment she let him go, turned, and without another word climbed on to the waiting train.

He stepped back, the feel of her kiss still on his lips. He was going to miss her, but he felt better with her out of the way. As dirty and nasty as this fight had gotten so far, he had no doubt it was about to get worse. And Anne didn't deserve to be in the way of it all.

By that evening, he had checked out of the Wallace Hotel. Just in case anyone was looking or would come asking, he made a public show of telling people where he was going.

He moved into a guest room on the second floor of the big house at Sharon's Dream. He figured there, anyone from the Brant ranch would have the most trouble getting close to him or his horse. And since he was going to make himself the target very soon in this fight, being as protected at night as possible was the best idea.

He had purposely missed Cain and Daniel's funeral that morning. And neither Hank nor Jim nor Walt had asked him about it. Fargo had never been much for funerals.

No one had moved into the big house besides him. Fargo guessed that none of them felt right doing so, and that was just fine. He felt odd himself, to tell the truth, wandering around in all of Cain's things, but right now this worked for a place to stay better than anywhere else he could think of.

He asked Hank, Jim, and Walt to join him for dinner to plan the next moves and to make sure the mine was set up with their security measures.

After an hour of talking over a rich beef stew, it was clear to Fargo that the new owners of Sharon's

Dream felt they were ready for just about anything anyone could throw at them. The problem was, they didn't really understand what was headed their way. They were mostly miners, solid men who didn't mind a fight, but who also weren't trained day after day in the business of fighting.

Brant had hired a lot of professionals, and chances were he would be hiring even more before this started. One thing Fargo was convinced of, no matter how prepared they were, the miners of Sharon's Dream were outmatched in a direct fight against professional trailsmen who were willing to kill to collect their day's pay.

Fargo was going to try to make sure that fight never got to them.

"Now," Fargo said, "I need to ask you one favor. I need a room in the stable secured on all sides and reinforced to hold someone. A prison cell. Can you do that? Make something easy to guard and escape proof?"

Jim looked at Hank, who was nodding. Finally Hank said, "Sure, when do you need it ready?"

"Tomorrow sometime, but it may not get used for a few days. It depends on how soon I can track down our future guest."

"Can I ask who that might be?" Hank said.

"No," Fargo replied. "I'll make it a surprise."

Fargo smiled. The stage was set. Now all he had to do was what he did best—track down his future prisoner, Sarah Brant.

Anne couldn't enjoy the train trip. She was worried about Fargo. She knew that he was in a battle he might lose. And pay for with his life. Friendship mattered to Fargo. Nothing would stop him.

The train offered the convenience of speed and the inconvenience of noisy children and irritating drummers who thought that their dubious charms just might get them a little fun when nighttime came and trysts were possible in certain parts of the passenger cars.

A man with a ginger mustache that extended at least an inch from both sides of his upper lip abruptly sat down next to her without permission or warning. His checkered suit and cheap cigar marked him as one of the standard-issue peddlers who roamed the West in pursuit of modest fortunes and immodest moments with as many women as they could get their hands on.

He looked over at her and smiled his cold rattlesnake smile and said, "Mind if I sit down?"

"Looks like you already have."

"Well, I guess I have at that." He tipped his derby. "Gil Fairbain. At your service. Very nice to meet you."

She stared at him a moment, not matching his greeting. "There are other seats you could be sitting in."

His smile revealed cheap false teeth. "But none with a beautiful woman in the seat beside me, madam."

Then she sat watching the foothills go by in the late afternoon.

Fairbain said, tapping his chest, "I've got some good rye here. A whole pint of it. If you'd care to have some."

"No, thanks." Still looking out the window.

"Well, then I guess I'll just have to drink alone." Silence between them for a time. Rattle and sway of train. Cry of babies. Foot slaps of older kids running up and down the aisle. She concentrated on the scenery. Shadows were forming now, lending the land a purple beauty. He concentrated on his bottle of rye. She could almost hear his mind working like a vast machine, trying to come up with some approach that would make her throw herself into his arms.

Finally, his brain seemed to have settled on a tack to take with this woman who was treating him so coldly. The rye likely helped to convince him that he was about to reap the rewards of his ingenuity.

Her neck stiff from looking out the window, she had to sit back and face forward. This was his call to action.

"You probably couldn't guess what I am."

She laughed. "A drummer who doesn't have the horse sense to quit pestering women who find him obnoxious?"

His inebriated state allowed him to brush away her nasty remark. He even smiled. "That's the disguise I use. Looking like a drummer. That's how I can travel around without the law getting me."

Out of boredom, she decided to tease him some more. "You're a famous bank robber?"

"Guess again."

"An Indian chief?"

"You're not being serious, madam. So I'll tell you and save you the trouble. I'm a gunfighter."

Oh, Lord, she thought, *he's going to try and convince me that beneath his flabby self beats the heart of a dangerous gunny.* She almost felt sorry for him. "You've killed a lot of men then?"

"That's right," he said, sitting up in his seat, stretching his shoulders as if his arms were massive and he needed more room. Pathetic. "A lot of men."

"That must be a scary calling. Facing down killers that way."

He touched the left side of his long mustache. "That's one thing I gave up a long time ago."

"Oh?"

"Being afraid. Nobody scares me now. Nobody."

She could have kissed him. Not because he was desirable but because he'd given her a way to get rid of him. "That's quite a statement. Nobody scares you."

"Well, you get that way after you've killed a lot of men."

"It's funny you're a gunfighter."

"Oh? Why's that?"

"That's what my lover is."

Faint concern shone in his brown eyes. "Is that so?"

"You ever heard of the Trailsman?"

"Sure," he said, "who hasn't?" Then, realizing the name she'd just dropped: "You know the Trailsman?"

"We're practically engaged. In fact, he's waiting for

me in San Francisco. I'll introduce you to him when we get there. I'll tell him all about all the men you've killed. I know most gunfighters would be afraid of him. But I'll bet you're not."

He offered no good-bye. He jammed his pint of rye back into his suit coat, tamped his derby down, and headed for another empty seat. The rest of the trip she sat blissfully alone.

It took Fargo less than twenty-four hours to track down Miss Brant. The entire town had heard about Cain's will, so he knew she and her father had heard the news as well. It appeared she had done exactly what Fargo had expected her to do. She had headed to Sacramento to hire more guns to work for her.

From a rock high on the ridge he watched her leave her ranch, riding in a two-seater black buggy with five guards. Ten minutes behind her, he and his Ovaro stallion hit the Placerville road to follow. Four miles down the trail, he cut off to a high ridge on the right, riding fast to get ahead of her.

The black buggy was pulled by two horses and she didn't seem to be in any hurry, instead deciding to take the bumps and turns in the road a little slower to smooth the ride. She sat comfortably on a padded bench behind a driver, shaded from the sunlight by a fold-up roof. Two guards on horseback in front of the buggy, two behind.

Fargo knew every inch of the Placerville road, and knew exactly the best place to capture the woman. And he got there easily ahead of her.

He stood waiting patiently behind a tall rock near the edge of the road as the buggy and riders approached.

The two lead riders passed him, their guns in leather, their carbines in sheaths. Obviously, no one in this group had been expecting trouble.

As the buggy came level with him, Fargo stepped from behind the boulder and said, "Lot more of you than there are of me. But I can take at least two of you out before you can get your guns out of their holsters."

"Fargo, you bastard," Sarah Brant snapped.

"Fargo?" one of the men said. "You mean the Trailsman?"

"He's not as tough as you'd think," she said, "and anyway, I don't pay you to be sissies."

Fargo saw that he had the edge, at least momentarily. They looked impressed with the man confronting them. Or at least, as Sarah Brant had implied, impressed with his reputation.

"One at a time, drop your guns, starting with you."

He nodded for the first lead rider to lift his six-shooter from his holster. Then he said, "Now the carbine."

"Some man you are," Sarah Brant said to the guard.

It took several minutes before the men were shorn of their weapons. Then Fargo said to the driver, "You stay." Then to the others he said, "I want all the rest of you to get the hell out of here."

"We're comin' back for you, mister," one man snapped.

"Bring some guts when you do."

Sarah Brant laughed at Fargo's joke. She enjoyed seeing these cowed men humiliated even more.

But the men rode off.

Fargo spoke to the driver. "Move the buggy slowly off the road this way, then get down and tie off the horses." Then he turned to the passenger. "Miss Brant, would you please remain seated and do not move. I would love to have an excuse to shoot you."

Fargo stayed to the side and in clear view of both of them as the driver moved the horses and buggy as he had been told to do.

"What do you want from me, Fargo?" Sarah Brant asked, her voice almost a hiss. "I've done nothing to you."

Her driver climbed down and tied off the horses. Fargo continued to make sure that he could see both of them every second.

"I have a bullet hole through me that says otherwise," Fargo said. "And you killed a good friend of mine and his son."

"I had nothing to do with any of that," she said, glaring at him.

"Of course you didn't," Fargo said. "I'm sure all of this was your father's idea."

She continued glaring and said nothing.

"Now, please step down from the buggy. Leave your bag."

"Why should I?" she asked.

"Because if you don't, I'll have to drag you down. And I don't think you'd like that."

Reluctantly, she stood and climbed to the ground.

He motioned that she should move over and stand beside her guard and she did. The guard stepped a half step away from her, glaring at her. Fargo had no idea what that was about, and didn't much care.

Fargo took a thin rope he had hanging from his belt and tossed it to the guard. "Tie her up, feet to her hands, nice and tight."

"I will not be trussed up like a common criminal," she said.

"But you are a common criminal," Fargo said. "Just because you're a woman doesn't excuse you from what you've done. Now sit down and let him tie you up."

"I will not."

He smirked at her. Then he walked over to her, slid his arm around her shoulders, and kicked her feet out from under her. He moved so quickly that she didn't have time to put up any kind of fight.

She looked like a humiliated little girl sitting next to her guard. Her cheeks flamed. Her lips formed unladylike words. Her eyes burned with rage.

Fargo bent down and started to tie her up, chuckling to himself, yanking the cord tight, making sure that she wouldn't get free.

"My father will kill you for this."

But Fargo's attention was now on the driver. He ignored Sarah Brant and her anger.

He glared at the driver and said, "How'd you get hooked up with somebody like this, anyway?"

The driver shrugged. "Well, first of all, she's not a bad-looking lady. And she's got a lot of money. But when they started talking about attacking Sharon's Dream, with you on the other side, I decided I was going to have no part of it. I was headed down the trail once I got to Sacramento. That is, if I could get away before she shot me in the back."

"Hand me your gun," Fargo said.

The driver handed it over, looking worried, and Fargo quickly dumped the shells out of the chamber, then handed the gun back to the driver. It was a special Colt with a nice handle that the man had clearly taken good care of.

"Thanks," the driver said, looking relieved. "It was a gift from a good friend from home and I wouldn't have liked losing it."

"Don't do anything stupid and you won't die with it on your hip today."

The man nodded.

Fargo stared at the driver. He didn't feel completely right about the man, but he couldn't put his finger on what was bothering him. He looked young, not more than midtwenties, but he had an air about him that gave Fargo a sense the kid had been some places and seen some things already.

"What's your name and what was she paying you?"

"Name's Kip. Twenty a month plus room and board."

"Would you work for Sharon's Dream for twenty-five?" Fargo asked.

"Tell him no, Kip," Sarah Brant snapped.

Kip smiled at her. "Doesn't look like you're in charge of me anymore, Miss Brant. I told you I didn't want any part of raiding Sharon's Dream. I had a couple good friends in that mine. Now's a good time to say good-bye."

"I'll have to check with the owners, but I'm sure something can be arranged," Fargo said. "I hope none of the men who took off were your friends."

Kip shook his head. "Those four would have rather shot you than look at you. Miss Brant was on her way into Sacramento to hire more of the same type."

Fargo had already figured that, but it was good to have it confirmed.

"My father's going to take care of you too, Kip."

"Sounds like your father's going to be mighty busy." Fargo grinned.

Miss Brant cursed, wiggling in the dirt, trying to get her bindings loose. They ignored her and pulled the buggy even farther off the trail and down behind some rocks where it would be completely hidden. Then they unhooked the horses and brought them back up to the road.

Miss Brant was sitting up and glaring at them. "Kip, how could you?" she demanded, clearly understanding that Kip had changed sides completely. "You are a lazy, no-good ball of horse shit, and I meant what I said about my father taking care of you."

Kip shrugged, then turned to Fargo. "Mind if I slug her once?"

"If she doesn't shut up." Fargo winked at him so Sarah Brant couldn't see. "Sure, be my guest."

"Great," Kip said. He winked back. "I've never heard this woman not yap on about one thing or another."

She started to open her mouth, then thought better of it and snapped it closed.

Kip stared down at her as he pounded his fist into his hand. "It's only a matter of time. Only a matter of time."

Again she opened her mouth, thought better of it, and closed it.

Fargo laughed and whistled for the Ovaro. A moment later his horse appeared and Fargo untied a tarp from its back.

Fargo spread out the tarp and the two of them rolled her up in it. She wasn't going to have a comfortable trip back to Sharon's Dream—that was for sure—but she would survive.

Kip tossed her over one of the horses and mounted the other himself.

With Kip leading, they headed back up the Placerville road. It would only be a matter of time until Sarah Brant saw her new home. And she wasn't going to like it one bit.

Sarah Brant proved to be nothing if not resilient. Given the fact that she was tarp-wrapped and tied down on a horse, most reasonable people would assume that she would be afraid. But being a prisoner didn't humble her at all. "I suppose you think you're in control of this situation now."

"Sure looks that way."

"Well, you're wrong. You have no idea how powerful my father is. How many men he has. And when he finds out that you've taken me, he'll make your life hell. And I promise you that."

Fargo laughed. Her voice shook as they traveled over rough road.

"I'm glad you find this funny, you bastard."

"If I wasn't in a hurry to lock you up, I'd stop right here and tan your hide."

"Big, bad Fargo. Not afraid of women. A very brave man."

They hit a rough patch. It shut her up. Temporarily. She groaned several times and cursed several times when the bouncing and jouncing got especially bad. Fargo grinned.

Then she started again. "You think you know everything, Fargo. You don't know anything. You're going to be damned surprised by the time this all plays out."

"You'll be the one who's surprised. You're going to see all your old man's plans go to hell. And then you're going to see him pay for killing Cain."

"My father only kills when he has to."

Fargo snorted. "Don't even bother trying to defend him. You just make me all the madder. So shut up now or I'll give you that tanning I told you about."

Something in his voice convinced her he was serious. She finally shut up.

8

As Hank, Kip, Walt, and Jim watched, Fargo released Sarah Brant from the tarp, using his foot to roll her over and over on the stable floor.

She came out dazed and clearly hurting.

She froze, lying on her back, her eyes wide, panting through her nose and mouth.

Then Fargo roughly stood her up. "Now hold still."

She nodded and he cut the ties that held her feet, then the ropes around her wrists. She did as she was told and held still, so he didn't nick her at all, which was a slight disappointment to him.

He spun her around and nudged her into the boarded-up stall that would be her prison for the near future.

"Perfect," Fargo said, and slammed the door closed as the men behind him laughed. "Make sure that's secure, and no matter how much she screams, don't open it."

Walt stepped forward and, with a smile, slammed down the bar that held the door tightly shut. "She's going nowhere."

They could hear her screaming, but the sound seemed faint as it came through the thick wood.

Right now, Fargo knew Cain would be laughing.

Kip shook his head. "You know, for the weeks that I worked for that bitch, I could only dream something like this would happen. Thank you." He turned to the rest. "I'm a damn good shot. I'll fight every step of the way with you for free just to repay you for that show."

"Welcome aboard," Hank said, stepping forward and shaking Kip's hand. "We're going to need you."

"Maybe, maybe not," Fargo said. "We've cut off one head of the snake. One more head and this war just might fizzle before it really starts."

"We can only hope," Walt said.

Fargo pointed to the door. "Two men at all times on guard duty, and two outside on the other side of the stall wall."

All four of them nodded and Fargo left, heading for his Ovaro. It was still early afternoon and the sun was beating down on the dirt and rocks. There was still time to take care of the next business, if he could do it. And if he could, this might end quickly. If not, a lot of men were going to die.

Twenty minutes later, he had his horse safely in a stable in town and was headed for the Benson Saloon. Fargo had been told that Brant spent his afternoons there drinking and playing poker.

Fargo planned on breaking that game up. He needed to get a read on Brant, to see if he was really the one in charge, or if his daughter had been pulling all the strings. And maybe, if Brant had only one or two guards with him, get Brant to pull a gun on him. Even though he wanted to, Fargo figured he couldn't very well just kill the man in cold blood. It needed to be a fair fight. Otherwise, Brant was just going to have to live a few hours longer.

As Fargo walked through the batwings and into the slightly cooler air of the Benson Saloon, a silence fell over the room. A half dozen hands moved slowly closer to the butts of their guns.

In that instant, Fargo calculated his chances. He'd be an easy target for several professional gunfighters. The thing was to be bold. And to be quick. Gaze locked with gaze as he met the eyes of the gunnies watching him. A few of the men smirked, but most just tried to get a sense of him. How quick, how good. Sometimes reputations got inflated. A good number of so-called gunnies found themselves crumpling to the ground at the hand of some local laborer they'd pushed a little too far in a saloon just like this one.

Fargo knew that one of them was going to try him. As he took a couple of steps toward the man he assumed was Henry Brant, he kept his eyes fixed on the hands of the gunfighters watching him. The bartender, a thickset bald man, had a sneer for him.

And then it happened. He saw the move only peripherally but that was enough. He went into a crouch and when the short, swarthy man had managed to pull his Colt about halfway out of its holster, Fargo fired.

The man screamed. His gun fell to the floor with a heavy, dead sound. He held his good hand over his bad one, the way a man does when something has burned him. He knew a good number of curses.

"This is your lucky day," Fargo said. "I probably should have killed you. But I'll let somebody else do that for me. You won't be doing any fast draws with that hand. Not again you won't."

A tall man with a fierce black beard looked as if he was about to draw down on Fargo. Fargo's hand hovered above his own gun. "You won't have the same luck your friend did. I'll kill you on the spot. So you better think it over."

The man didn't like being cowed this way. But he obviously had only two choices. Take the humiliation that would come from backing down or fight Fargo. And he was wise enough to know that however many gunfights he'd survived in the past, his luck was about to run out. All of a sudden humiliation didn't sound so bad. He pulled his hand away from his gun.

The saloon girl sitting nearby in a soiled red dress obviously liked what she saw. Her ruby lips quirked in an inviting smile. She couldn't be sure if Fargo saw it.

It seemed everyone in the room knew who he was, and everyone in the room seemed to be on the other side. Ten men, plus the bartender.

He'd made it this far. Now he had to get down to business.

At a poker table in the corner, a silver-haired man

looked up from his cards and laughed. He looked powerful and very much in control of the room.

Henry Brant. There could be no doubt. And by the looks of this room, it was clear that Henry Brant paid the wages of every man here. He was far more powerful than his daughter.

"Well, well, it seems we have a famous guest in our presence. Fargo, what task brings you to us this fine afternoon? I heard you had moved in with that bunch at Cain's old mine."

Fargo stayed close to the batwings. If more guns cleared leather, his only hope was to dive backward and out the door. But before he did, he'd make sure to put a shot or two into Brant.

"I just wanted to meet the man who ordered the killing of my friend Cain Parker and his son."

A number of hands around the room edged even closer to their guns, but Brant just laughed, holding his hands up in the air in front of him to calm the men. "I had nothing to do with those unfortunate deaths, I can assure you."

Fargo said nothing in return. He just let Brant's laugh die off into silence.

Finally, Brant sat a little more upright in his chair and glanced at the cards in front of him. "Now that we have that cleared up, do you mind? You're interrupting my afternoon poker game."

"Not at all," Fargo said, moving one step closer to the door without turning his back on the room. "I just like to know what a man's face looks like before I kill him. You'll never know when I'll be there, Brant. Cain Parker was a good man. He didn't deserve to die. But you do. Very soon."

With that, Fargo stepped backward out of the door and to one side just in case anyone got the bright idea to shoot out the batwings at him.

Fargo walked down the street and around the block. He quickly ducked into a hotel lobby and up the staircase to the second floor. He knew that a window at the end of the upstairs hall looked out over the street in front of the Benson Saloon, and that's exactly where he wanted to be to see what happened next. He figured he wasn't going to have long to wait.

He was right. Ten minutes later, Brant came out, surrounded by six men.

The white-haired man looked nervous, glancing constantly up and down the busy street as they moved to their horses tied at the hitching posts in front of the saloon. A moment later, Brant and his men were headed out of town at full gallop. More than likely, there wouldn't be another poker game in the Benson real soon. And that was just fine by Fargo.

And Fargo had delivered the message to Brant that he had wanted to deliver. A man like him, afraid for his life, often made poor decisions. Fargo was counting on Brant to make more than his share of bad ones. And when he learned his daughter was missing, all hell was going to break loose.

But before that happened, it was time for Fargo to let loose a little hell of his own on Brant and his mine.

And with some luck, chase off anyone who really didn't want to work and die for the man.

The next morning, after a good night's rest in the guest room of Cain's big house, Fargo went to visit Sarah Brant. He carried a loaf of bread and a canteen full of water. He didn't want her dying in there just yet. But the longer she suffered, the happier he would be. You don't kill a good friend of the Trailsman and not live to regret it.

Walt and another man Fargo didn't recognize were on guard duty inside the stable. "Has the door been opened?"

"Nope," Walt said. "They tell me she stopped shouting sometime around midnight."

"Open it," Fargo said, "and keep a rifle trained on her."

Walt removed the board and pushed open the thick door.

The smell coming from the room flooded out and

washed over Fargo, making him smile at how she was suffering. She deserved it, every minute of it.

The light from the stable filled the cell and Fargo could see Sarah Brant sitting in one corner, her legs pulled up against her chest.

She looked up at him and blinked. Then she asked softly, "Why did you do this to me?"

"Why did you kill Cain, those other men, and finally Daniel? You know, don't you, that your boyfriend, Daniel, died sitting in an outhouse, afraid of you, afraid you were coming after him to kill him? And it seems he was right."

She looked up at Fargo and blinked. "I didn't know that. I honestly didn't."

Fargo laughed. "All the men I've talked to said you hired them, you gave the orders."

"I hired the men," she said. "My father said I was good at getting the right type of men to work for him. But I didn't hire them to kill Daniel." Her voice sounded more like a little girl's every moment. "I actually loved him. He was like a big puppy around me, and I adored that about him. I hoped to marry him. Why would I kill him?"

With that she broke down crying.

"So you're saying your father ordered Daniel's death?" Fargo asked, doubting that the show of tears was real.

"I don't know," she said between sobs. "Maybe. Or maybe Kip. I honestly don't know."

"Kip? Your driver?"

"My father's main foreman," she said, holding back the sobbing a little. "Kip was in love with me too and he hated Daniel, hated him with a passion, and hated me for loving Daniel. My father made Kip go everywhere with me as my personal bodyguard, and more than once I caught him spying on me and Daniel in a private moment."

Fargo's stomach twisted hard. Could she actually be telling the truth? More than likely, she was just playing him to get back at a man who had betrayed her. He glanced at Walt, who just shrugged.

"Thanks for the information, Miss Brant," Fargo said as he tossed in the loaf of bread. Then he tossed in the canteen and she caught that.

He motioned for Walt to close the door and bar it again.

The door slammed on her scream, muffling it like someone had put a pillow over her face.

Fargo turned to Walt. "Find Kip and bring him to me in the house."

Thirty minutes later, Walt came back, shaking his head. "No one has seen him since sunrise."

Fargo wanted to break something. He sure hoped he hadn't been taken in by Kip. If he had been, Kip would have told Henry Brant where his daughter was and how she was being held. And he would be getting ready to come after her.

"Get Hank and Jim in here as fast as you can. We've got to make some defense plans."

Walt turned and headed out the door at a run.

Fargo dropped into a chair in Cain's dining room. The war was about to start, and it was going to get deadly very fast.

And he didn't have any idea how to stop it now.

9

After a quick planning session with Hank, Walt, and Jim, Fargo headed back to the stable with Jim. He opened the door to Sarah Brant's prison and said clearly and firmly, "Come with me."

She stood on shaky legs and moved toward the stall door, almost slipping and falling twice before she got into the main stable area.

"Why are you letting me go?" she asked, looking stunned.

"I'm not, really," Fargo said. "I'm just giving you back to your father to protect for the moment. By tomorrow morning, I expect you to be in Sacramento boarding the first train available going east."

She stared at him and said nothing, so he went on.

"I want you out of this whole situation. You understand me?"

"Completely," she said, shivering. "But you still didn't answer my question."

He stared into her dark eyes. "Because Daniel and Cain would have wanted me to."

For a moment she looked confused, then nodded. "You're right. Thank you. I'll be on that train and never leave the East Coast again."

"And you might try to convince your father before you leave that trying to take over the Sharon's Dream mine is a fool's mission."

She quickly mounted the horse and then looked

down at Fargo. "My father has never listened to me before. I don't expect he will now."

She turned the horse and headed toward her father's mine, cutting up through the rocks and over the lower part of the ridge instead of going down the road.

"Do you think you bought us some time?" Jim asked from beside Fargo.

"Maybe a little. Depends on if she leaves or not."

"She's not leaving," Jim said.

"She's not leaving," Walt agreed.

Fargo watched her disappear over the hill. He wasn't so sure about that. But it seemed that lately he had been wrong about people a great deal. And that wasn't like him.

The expected attack from the Brant mine didn't come that afternoon, so work in the Sharon's Dream mine went back to normal, with guards doubled on the ridgeline and around the other entrances to the compound.

An hour before sunset, Fargo had gone with Jim high up on the ridge with a spyglass. They had taken turns watching the Brant mine and compound. It seemed like a normal evening down there.

A long time ago, when Cain and Brant still pretended to get along, Jim had visited the Brant mine. He slowly gave Fargo a tour of the compound, where the mine entrance was in relationship to the bunkhouses, how far it was from building to building, approximately how many men were working there. He even had a rough floor plan of the big ranch house that spread along a shallow ridgeline.

From their vantage point high up, Fargo spotted at least a half dozen guards in posts around the compound. But beyond that it looked like normal activity in and out of the mine. There didn't seem to be any attack being planned at all. And that made no sense. What was he missing?

Fargo studied what he could see of the trail leading up to the mine entrance on the hillside under them. In fact, the entire mountain they were on was honeycombed with both Sharon's Dream and Brant's tunnels.

"How close do you think they are from breaking through into one of our tunnels?" Fargo asked.

"The men haven't heard anything on any shift," Jim said. "And trust me, they're all listening."

Fargo shook his head. This entire fight, the reason Cain and Daniel were killed, was the gold ore. Brant's mine was petering out while Sharon's Dream was still following thick veins. Everything came back to the gold. Brant had to be going after the gold first. He didn't care about the buildings or the people, only the gold. He would go after the gold first, the miners second.

Fargo turned from the spyglass to look at Jim. "Gold mine tunnels have a lot of false lead tunnels and short side tunnels, am I right?"

"You're right. A number of them of varied lengths."

"Have you checked all those dead-end tunnels?"

Jim nodded. "They're all boarded off."

"Easy to break through boards," Fargo said as he watched yet another man carry a large wooden case up toward the mine. It looked like an ammunition case.

Jim said nothing and after a few seconds, Fargo again looked away from the spyglass and at Jim.

"It's possible they're coming that way," Jim said after a moment. "Two of those side tunnels are long and go toward the Brant mine."

"Can you blow the entrances to those side tunnels closed without bringing down the entire mine?"

Jim nodded. "We can, and we have to do it *now*."

"My thoughts exactly," Fargo said, standing a half beat behind Jim and following him at a near run down the ridge.

One hour later they had the mine empty and a team starting to blow the side tunnels, all of them that could hook up with any Brant tunnel.

Twenty minutes before midnight, Jim came out of the entrance to the mine, his face covered in dark dust. Fargo was standing there with a dozen others, waiting, watching.

"We got them all blown shut. You were right. We heard voices down one tunnel right before we blew it. Now it would take a dozen men a week to open any of them back up, and if they tried, we'd hear them."

"Good," Fargo said. "Now to get to the gold, they have to come at us where we can see them. Have everyone standing by for an attack at dawn."

Fargo turned and headed into the dark.

"Where are you going?" Jim asked.

Without turning around, Fargo said, "I'm going to try to reduce the numbers on the other side a little. No matter what you hear, stay here and be ready for a possible attack at dawn. Brant and his men are coming to take your mine away from you."

"Not likely," Fargo heard Jim mutter behind him.

Fargo didn't want to tell him that it *was* likely. Very likely. The coming fight was between miners and the professional fighters and gunhands Brant had hired. It wouldn't be a fair fight at all unless Fargo could change the odds a little. And he had about eight hours of darkness to do just that.

Slowly, silently, Fargo worked his way over and around the rocks toward the guard positions set up by Brant around his compound. Fargo had no real idea how long it took him to get to them, but once he crossed the ridgeline and was on Brant's side of the hill, he avoided looking into the lights of the Brant mine compound to make sure his night vision stayed as good as it could be. They had the place lit up with at least three dozen lanterns hanging from poles and the sides of buildings.

Fargo found the first guard right where he had spotted him from high on the mountain. He had his carbine across his lap and was sipping on a cup of something that smelled of beef.

Fargo slammed the butt of the Henry into the man's head with so much force that the guard's hat flew off and blood began leaking from his ear.

The man's carbine rattled to the ground on the rocks and Fargo eased him to the dirt.

"What's the matter, Ray?" a voice said from out of the dark about fifty paces away. "Can't hold on to your gun while you piss?"

Fargo grunted loudly as if in response to the man's question.

The man laughed and went silent.

Fargo checked out the man at his feet. He was a professional, and Fargo remembered seeing his face on a wanted poster down south. His name had been Ray Tanner. From what Fargo knew about him, he usually worked with his brother Carl. More than likely, it was Carl who had kidded him.

Fargo moved over toward the second guard, taking his time, making sure that no footstep he took made a sound, pausing between every step, staying low and undercover behind the large rocks where he could.

In the dim light, he could see the guard sitting on a flat rock, his carbine also across his legs.

As Fargo eased closer, the man turned and whispered loudly into the night. "Hey, Ray, how much time do we have left?"

At that moment, two men appeared from a bunkhouse below and the man said, "Never mind. Put your watch back in your pocket. I see them coming."

Fargo took one quick step toward the man and hit him full force. The man groaned and slipped, unconscious, to the ground.

Fargo, with the same movement, grabbed the man's carbine so it didn't go clattering into the rocks.

He eased the man down and then watched as the two men started up the hill toward the guard positions.

It was doubtful he could take them both out silently. It looked like it was time for a change of plans. A more direct approach worked better for him anyway.

He took his Henry from over his shoulder and made

sure a cartridge was in the chamber. He needed two shots in quick succession to make this work.

The two guards were now climbing up on a narrow trail toward him. He killed the one in front first, then killed the second guard before the gunhand even had time to go for his gun or duck behind a rock.

Taking the first guard's ammunition belt, Fargo headed back up and into the rocks, moving quickly now, the sounds covered by all the commotion in the yard caused by his shots.

He found a large boulder for cover and locked new cartridges into the chambers of the Henry. There was no guard between him and the ridgeline back to Sharon's Dream if he needed to make a hasty retreat. The Brant guards that he knew about were all below and beside him. This was as good a location as any to get a little target practice.

Below, a number of men were moving around in the light, shouting orders. Fargo ignored the men who looked like miners and worked to spot the professionals.

Picking one who seemed to be in charge, he shot him through the chest. Fargo's gun cracked loudly in the night air, and he knew it spit just enough fire to let someone who was watching pinpoint his location.

The man he had shot slammed into the side of a bunkhouse, fired one shot into the air, and then went down hard, clutching his chest. No one went to help him and after a moment he stopped moving.

Fargo stayed perfectly still as the men below all took cover and tried to figure out exactly where the shot had come from.

The miners, not used to a fight, ran for the bunkhouses and the mine tunnel. It was the professionals who stayed, rifles in hand, taking any cover they could, waiting for Fargo to make the next move.

Fargo figured he could outwait them. They didn't know exactly where he was on the pitch-dark hillside and he could more or less see all of them in the lights from his high position in the rocks.

He silently put another shell into his carbine, then lay against the rock, holding his fire and watching.

Finally, one man moved, running low toward the trail that led up into the rocks. The idiot figured he would outflank Fargo by climbing directly up the rocks at him.

The man paid for his stupid thinking as Fargo caught him in midstride and he tumbled like those people you see in a circus act. Except this one didn't come up onto his feet and never would again.

Again, there was silence over the compound.

Fargo moved silently over to another rock on the left about twenty paces away and reloaded. Then he went back to watching the scene below.

Through the window of the big house, Fargo caught a glimpse of a man's shadow.

Fargo sent a shot through the window, exploding glass inward like a kid had hit it with a rock. He doubted he had hit Brant, unless he'd gotten lucky. But if that had been Brant standing there, he'd at least been cut by the flying glass.

From the yard below, a man shouted up at him. "Fargo, is that you? We have no fight with you."

"You do as long as you work for Henry Brant," Fargo replied, turning his head toward the right and shouting back at the mountain to let the echoes confuse them as to his exact location. "Go to the stable and mount up and ride right now and I'll let you live." Fargo again shouted at the mountain to his right.

His voice echoed over the compound and then silence filled the dark night again.

Suddenly, one man near a horse trough started firing at the lanterns hanging around the compound, hitting one, missing another, trying to put the compound into darkness.

Fargo ducked down and moved to yet another large rock, putting another shell in the carbine as he went.

"Offer still stands!" he shouted, this time at the rocks and steep hillside to his left.

A good two dozen miners poured out of the mine

entrance and headed down the trail at a fast run. More poured out of the bunkhouse.

"Stop!" one of the men in the courtyard shouted at them and raised his gun. The idiot was ready to fire on his own men. Fargo shook his head at the stupidity of it.

Fargo put a bullet through the edge of the wall the man was hiding against and into the man's gut before he had a chance to shoot at any of the fleeing miners.

The shot made the miners run faster and within twenty seconds, they had all poured into the stable and out of sight.

Fargo again moved to a different firing position as he pushed another shell into the chamber, staying silent and low in the dark. No one below wanted to risk a blind shot up into the rocks for fear of drawing his fire. He had them pinned down and scared and without a leader. Still, the men down there were professionals, and Fargo decided that being safe and continuing to move was the best plan.

A few minutes of silence in the standoff before suddenly the farside stable doors burst open and the fleeing miners headed down the road, most of them in a large wagon, a few on horseback riding ahead and carrying lanterns.

It seemed that Brant had lost a large part of his fighting force. But Fargo figured there were still a good twenty to thirty professional guns left down there, some pinned down in the courtyard, some in the buildings. If he had to go through all of them to get to Henry Brant, he would.

He turned and shouted into the rocks next to him.

"Time's up on the offer."

Two of the guards still holding stations in the rocks above the compound opened up on his position, bouncing lead off the rocks around him.

Fargo slid back into cover. Crouching, he ran along the rocks, moving silently to yet another area of cover, this one farther up on the hill so that he had a better angle on the guards in the rocks.

He didn't dare end up trapped on this hillside in the light, not with so many professional guns facing him. So he was forced to move back up and over the ridge while it was still dark enough for cover.

As the sun finally showed a little light in the sky, a signal that the day would be clear and again hot, Fargo walked between two of the miners guarding Sharon's Dream and down toward the big white building where Jim and Walt and Hank were waiting on the porch holding carbines on their laps.

All three stood as he approached.

"Sounds like you were busy," Jim said, smiling.

Hank said, "And our guards above the entrance to Brant's mine told us that a large group of miners, in fact most of them who worked for Brant, beat a hasty retreat headed for Sacramento about one in the morning."

"There's still a lot of professional guns over there," Fargo said, stepping up onto the porch. "I need to get back up on the hill and watch what's going on, but I thought I'd come first for a little breakfast before it got too light."

"We figured you might," Walt said. "Got the cooks up early, as if any of us could sleep with the gunfire going on."

Fargo nodded. "At least for the moment, they're not coming this way. Now I have to stop them from ever coming this way."

"And how do you plan on doing that?" Hank asked as they all went inside.

"By cutting off the head of the snake," Fargo said. He smiled at Hank. "Haven't you been listening?"

10

By the time the sun was just starting to light up the tallest peaks of the mountains, Fargo, with Jim at his side, was back high on the ridgeline with the spyglass, watching the Brant compound. The food and the morning light had cleared some of the tiredness that had started to set in his bones during the last few hours of his attack on the compound. He knew he could go a couple of days without sleep. He had done so in the past, but he didn't like it, and he worried about what no sleep did to his judgment and speed. He wanted to get this finished today. One way or another.

The bodies still lay where he had shot them, but as the light filled the sky, the men were starting to move around in the compound a little.

"Fargo, I'm impressed," Jim said, staring through the eyepiece. "You really cut their numbers down. So, what do you think their next play is?" He handed Fargo the spyglass.

A number of men were now starting to pull the bodies around behind the stable and toward the small mine cemetery.

"We've cut off his plan on taking over the mine through his mine," Fargo said. "And he doesn't have enough men to stage a direct attack anymore. So he needs to hire more, which is what I think he will do."

"And we're not going to allow him to go do that, are we?" Jim asked, laughing.

"No, we're not," Fargo said.

Below, he saw the familiar figure of Kip moving around the yard, barking orders. That kid was going to die and die ugly. Fargo was going to make sure of that. No one tricked him like Kip had done and got away with it.

Fargo handed Jim the spyglass and said, "Look who showed his ugly face."

Jim stared for a moment, then shook his head and handed the glass back to Fargo. "The kid had us all fooled."

Fargo said nothing. His impulse was to ride into the compound and kill Brant and Kip. But it was better to keep his rage under control.

A few minutes later, Brant came out on the porch of the big house followed by his daughter. He had a bandage on one side of his forehead that made Fargo smile. He hadn't killed the man in the window last night, but he had clearly got him with the glass.

Sarah Brant looked like she was back to normal. She seemed to have no intention of leaving anytime soon. She was talking to her father and watching the activity in the courtyard.

Fargo watched as Kip moved over to them and said something, and both Brant and his daughter laughed.

After twenty minutes, Brant and his daughter turned and went back into the house arm in arm. Kip kept the men working, cleaning up the area, posting new guards, moving the bodies.

No one made a motion to leave, and no one new came up the road.

After two hours of watching as the sun warmed the air around them, Fargo sat up from his position flat on a rock surface and shook his head. "They're waiting for something."

"That's my sense as well," Jim said. "But for what?"

"I don't know," Fargo said. And that bothered him something awful. Again, Brant seemed to be a step ahead of him.

What were they waiting for?

Henry Brant was ruthless and only after the ore.

He didn't care about people or who died for him or against him. Only the gold mattered. And now he needed more men to get to the gold.

So somehow, he already had more men coming.

But he also needed something to take care of Fargo, to take him out of the picture in one fashion or another.

The beautiful image of Anne lying there naked in that bathtub snapped into his mind and his stomach twisted into a tight knot. Suddenly, he had an urgent need to know if Anne was all right.

He jumped to his feet. "Keep as many eyes as possible on that compound and the road leading into it," he said to Jim. "Don't start a fight unless you have to until I get back."

Jim stood. "What's happening? Where are you going?"

Fargo stared one last time down at the Brant compound. "I think I know what they're waiting for and I need to make sure both things don't get here."

With that, he turned and headed off down the hill at a steady run, trying to keep his fear in check, trying to push the image of Anne tied up and beaten from his mind. After what he had done to Sarah Brant, he couldn't imagine what those two would do with Anne if they got her inside that building down there.

"When will you be back?" Jim shouted after him.

"As soon as I can," Fargo shouted back.

As soon as he made sure Anne was safe. But his gut told him that he was already too late.

He rode the Ovaro hard and fast down the Placerville road, keeping his head low as he slashed past wagons and other riders.

In record time, he reached the telegraph office in Sacramento and had them wire an urgent message to Anne at her hotel in San Francisco. He paid extra to have the message run to her and a response brought back as quickly as possible.

While he waited, he headed for Marshal Davis's office. He usually liked to go it alone and didn't often feel he needed help, but right now he did. If Anne had been taken, he didn't care how many people helped him get her back. All that was important was that she was safe.

"Fargo," Marshal Davis said, smiling as Fargo entered the office. "Glad to see you're still alive and kicking."

"I do my best," Fargo said.

"I hear it's a real hornet's nest up there right now. Even the Placerville sheriff is staying out of the way."

"It might get worse before it gets better if I can't get something stopped here real quick."

He explained to the marshal everything that had happened so far, then told him the two reasons why he was in town.

"You think they'll go after her?" Marshal Davis asked.

"I'm getting to know how Henry Brant thinks. He needs me out of the way to get the Sharon's Dream gold. And people around Placerville have seen me with Anne, so he knows she means something to me. He'll go after that leverage on me. That's why I had her leave town in the first place, but my guess is he had her followed, or had someone track her down."

"Makes sense," the marshal said, grabbing his hat and heading for the door. "Let's go see if you have a telegram back yet."

As they entered the office, the telegram came in, and it was exactly what Fargo had feared the most. Anne had checked out suddenly this morning.

Fargo stared at the telegram, trying to control the twisting dread in his stomach, then handed the slip of paper to the marshal.

"She wouldn't do that," Fargo said.

The marshal nodded, then glanced at the clock on the wall. "First train in from San Francisco is in twenty minutes. That would be the quickest way to bring her in. Otherwise it would take a good day of riding around the bay. Let me round up some deputies and we'll meet it. They won't suspect we're coming."

112

Fargo nodded his thanks. "You might want to have as many men as you can get. Brant has reinforcements coming in as well. Gunhands. My guess is many of them are wanted men. They all might be coming in together."

"Meet you at the train station," Marshal Davis said and headed out the door at a fast trot.

Fargo stared for a moment longer at the telegram, then flipped it back on the counter.

Cain dead, his son dead, now Anne taken. How much worse could this get?

He decided he didn't want an answer to that question.

11

He found a place against the stone wall of the train station, right in the middle, his back to a door into a luggage area. The door had a window in it head-high for people to see in or out as they went through.

The train was starting to pull in as the marshal arrived, spreading out his men along the platform. There were enough other people on the platform that the marshal's men blended in pretty well.

Fargo stepped back inside the door to the luggage area. No point in taking a chance that someone on the train would recognize him before they got off. His only chance against professional gunhands with this many people around was to catch them by surprise.

That was also the only way to make sure Anne got away safely.

Steam from the locomotive flooded the platform as it passed, its wheels grinding as it braked slowly to a stop.

Fargo noticed that the marshal also had men moving along the tracks to the area where the baggage and animal cars would stop, moving casually as if nothing was wrong. Fargo was impressed. In a very short time he had talked to his deputies and had them trained for the situation. The marshal was even more competent than Fargo had thought.

Fargo stared through the tiny door window at the windows of the first passenger car as it eased slowly past him.

No Anne. More than likely she would be in one of the cars surrounded by five or six men.

The five passenger cars slowly ground to a very noisy halt in front of Fargo, the middle one not more than twenty paces from him through the growing crowd.

So far, he hadn't seen Anne in any of the first three cars.

He stepped from the door as the people inside the cars stood and started to get off. He kept his hat pulled down and his shoulders hunched to avoid being recognized.

It was from the fourth car that a man carrying a leather rifle pouch got off and looked around, scanning the crowd before stepping to the platform.

Mick Rule.

Fargo knew that face very well. He had hoped to never have a run-in with the man. He was fast and deadly with a gun, almost as deadly as Fargo was.

Rule was also wanted in three states. He had robbed banks, killed guards and lawmen, and was known to work with a dozen other men. It was no wonder Henry Brant had been waiting. It was no wonder Sarah Brant hadn't left as Fargo had told her to do. With Rule and his men headed their way, they could control not only Sharon's Dream, but more than likely a lot of Placerville.

Two more men got off behind Rule, followed by Anne. Fargo's jaw clenched as he saw how she was being shoved around.

The marshal and his men had seen Rule as well, but were still holding their positions, hoping to let some of the crowd thin.

Fargo didn't much care about the crowd.

But he did care about getting Anne out of the way of those men unharmed, and that meant waiting for the right time to attack.

Eight men total climbed off the train and moved out of the way, shoving Anne along with them.

She looked angry. Damned angry. He had seen that look on her face only once before, the day she found out two of her most trusted men were working to take over her ranch.

The outlaws stood for a moment in a small circle on the platform, talking, waiting for something as the crowd started to climb onto the train. It would be only a moment before the marshal and his men would stand out like sore thumbs to the outlaws.

He had only six shots in his Colt. If he made the play, he was going to have to hope the marshal and his men took care of at least two of the outlaws. Otherwise he was going to end up very dead right here on this train platform.

Fargo took a deep breath and stepped toward the men, his Colt heavy in his hand at his side. Out of the corner of his eye, he saw the marshal nod and step toward the group as well.

At least two guns against eight.

The odds were getting slightly better.

This was going to have to be quick and deadly. There was no other way.

Ten paces away from the group of eight men, with no stray passenger between him and the man who held Anne by the arm, Fargo said loudly, "Excuse me. I think you're holding a friend of mine."

Mick Rule smirked at Fargo. His grasp on Anne's arm tightened.

"I don't think you want to draw down on me, Fargo. You've got a big reputation but I've got the speed."

Rule leaned away from Anne so that he could get at his gun. He was fast all right. But not fast enough for Fargo. Rule got one shot off but by that time Fargo had put a bullet in the heavy man's heart.

Rule went down hard, his head smashing into the platform.

Anne spun away and fell to the deck, covering her head as other passengers around them screamed and also dove for cover.

At the same time, Marshal Davis cut two more of

the outlaws down and the deputies cleared off the rest of them.

The sound of the shots and the cries of the passengers were still echoing as Marshal Davis turned to see five more gunnies jumping from the rail car that held the horses.

This battle was even bloodier than the first one but lasted for less than twenty seconds. It was fought in front of the baggage and cattle cars. Davis lost two deputies but only one gunny survived.

Fargo glanced around as the smoke from the guns cleared. People were flat on the platform or crouched behind luggage. From what he could see, none of the bystanders had been wounded. That was the first good thing that had happened in two days.

He leathered his Colt and reached down and offered a hand to Anne, who was still on the platform, staying low until she was sure the gunfire had ended.

"It's over," Fargo said.

Behind him, the marshal and his deputies surrounded the pile of dead outlaws. The deputies checked the shot men while the marshal started to work on calming the crowd.

"It's over, everyone," he shouted up and down the platform. "It's safe to board the train and go about your business. Sorry for the problem this morning."

Anne looked up at Fargo, her eyes blazing in anger. "How did you know?"

"I tend to keep track of the people I care about," he said.

She slowly took his offered hand and let him help her gently to her feet.

"Are you hurt?" he asked.

She shook her head, brushing off her skirt, trying to straighten herself a little as she gathered her wits about her.

"Did you get my shirt?"

She still looked somewhat dazed from all the gunplay. But she smiled and said, "I didn't have time to get you a shirt, Skye. But I did bring you a nice little surprise I think you'll like." She slid her hand in his. "And I think you'll like it a lot more than a shirt."

He laughed. "Yeah, I think I will too."

12

Fargo was in no hurry to get back to Sharon's Dream.

He helped Anne give a statement to the marshal, then escorted her to the Sacramento Inn, a large and plush hotel near the marshal's office. They went to the dining room for a leisurely and quiet lunch. They had some talking to do before they headed back to Placerville.

As they waited for their order to come, Fargo said, "You look mad."

"I am mad," she said, her green eyes flashing. "I agreed to go to San Francisco to avoid this very thing, and it followed me there, where I had no one to help me, no one who knew me, no way to fight and defend myself."

"I know," he said. "And I'm sorry."

She shook her head. "Not your fault. Look, I've been defending myself for years now. I should have just stayed in my hotel and fought if I had to."

He nodded. "I agree."

She looked at him, puzzled, not expecting that answer from him.

"You can take care of yourself. I like that in a woman."

She squeezed his hand and smiled, a tear forming in the corner of her eye. "Thank you."

She took a deep breath, straightened up, and then said, "Besides a few bruises on my arms, I wasn't harmed. They caught me as I came out of my room, put a gun on me, and told me to pack and check out.

I did what they said, figuring I'd wait for my chance to break away. That, thanks to you, never came."

"Did you know any of them?" Fargo asked.

She shook her head, so he told her. "The leader was Mick Rule."

Her face went pale. "The bank robber and killer?"

"The same one. Henry Brant hired him and his men to help them take over Sharon's Dream."

She shuddered slightly. "Okay, I can take care of myself, but Mick Rule is out of my league. Thank you for rescuing me. You still didn't tell me how you knew I was in trouble."

"When you've been on the trail as many years as I have, you learn to trust your gut. My gut told me you were in trouble."

She shook her head, not understanding. "Sometimes, Fargo, you puzzle me."

At that moment the food came. After the waiter left, she said, "Start from the beginning and tell me everything that's happened so far."

He managed to keep things simple. Clean and clear. Her expression changed from time to time as he told her about the gunfights and his suspicions where the Brants were concerned.

"Now what, Skye?"

"Dessert," Fargo said.

Anne laughed. Fargo smiled, enjoying the sound. He had been afraid this morning that he would never hear that laugh again.

"After dessert, silly."

"We check in with the marshal to make sure he doesn't need anything more from us; then we get you a horse and take a nice, peaceful ride back to the Wallace Hotel."

"Aren't you afraid Henry Brant is going to hear that he has no help coming, and that I'm safe?"

"I hope so," Fargo said.

Again, she looked puzzled. Then she smiled. "Oh, I see. You're thinking the gunhands still with him will hear they're on their own and they'll abandon the sinking ship."

Fargo nodded, finishing off his sandwich and downing the last of his glass of water.

"And then Henry and Sarah Brant will make a run for it," Anne said, smiling. "And you will track them down and deliver the justice they so deserve."

"And my friend's mine will be safe," Fargo said. "That's my hope. But with many things concerning Brant, I haven't guessed right. We'll just have to go back and see."

"Good," she said. "I miss my bed and my bathtub."

Fargo smiled. "Interestingly enough, I miss your bed and your bathtub too."

"Well," she said, "when this is over, we'll have to solve that problem."

As the sun burned down directly on them, they headed back up the Placerville road, moving at a comfortable pace. It was still an hour before sunset when they reached Anne's hotel. After they had her things back in her room, they both went to talk to Reg.

Fargo filled him in on the threat to Anne, and the three of them made plans to set up extra security around the hotel and at night around her room.

"Don't expect help from the sheriff here," Fargo said at one point. "Marshal Davis told me that his way of dealing with situations like this is to stay out of the way."

"We've already noticed that," Anne said.

After Fargo was comfortable that Anne and Reg had the hotel protected fairly well, he headed back out to the mine.

Men from Sharon's Dream stood guard over both the road to their own mine and the road to the Brant mine.

Hank, Jim, and Walt met him as he rode up and into the stable to take care of his horse. As he unsaddled the big stallion and rubbed him down before giving him some grain, he told the three what had happened in Sacramento.

"Mick Rule?" Hank said, his eyes going wide when Fargo mentioned the name. "If he and his gang join Brant, we won't stand a chance."

"No worry about that now," Fargo said. "He's dead, as are most of his men. And Anne is safe and sound in the Wallace for the night."

"Dead?" Walt asked. "You killed Mick Rule?"

Fargo shrugged as he finished with his horse and turned to face the three mine owners. "Marshal Davis and his deputies were in the fight as well. Has anyone gone in or out of the Brant mine?"

"No one," Walt said. "No one has even tried."

"We've had a dozen sets of eyes on the compound at all times," Hank said, "and nothing has happened over there besides their changing the guard every few hours. They just seem to be waiting."

"For Mick Rule and his men to bring Anne to them," Jim said.

Fargo didn't know what to think now. He had gone under the assumption that Brant would know by now about what had happened in Sacramento. But maybe the fact that he didn't would be an advantage for a short time.

"Get more men on the road into Brant's mine. Don't let anyone in."

Hank turned and headed out of the stable to give the order. Jim and Walt and Fargo followed.

Fargo doubted that Brant and his men would allow themselves to be pinned down like Fargo had done to them last night. But there might be other ways to cause them a long, sleepless night while they waited for help that was no longer coming.

Fargo headed for the main house and the dining room. What he had in mind was going to take a little planning, but if it worked, Brant and his daughter and Kip were going to be very tired and very angry by tomorrow morning.

* * *

Fargo sat at the big table in Cain's dining room, staring at the huge chandelier, thinking and waiting for Hank, Jim, and Walt to join him.

When they did, Hank confirmed that there were now twenty armed men guarding the entrance and any other way down into Brant's mine compound and no one had yet tried to pass.

"Good," Fargo said.

"Best defense is a good offense," Hank said, nodding. "An ancient fact of war."

"And that's exactly what this damned thing is," Fargo said. "A war."

"We know that," Walt said. "We're not going anywhere."

Fargo raised his hand. "I didn't say you were. And I appreciate you throwin' in with me."

All three men nodded.

Fargo said, "How much dynamite do you have?"

"This is a mine," Hank said. "We normally have a lot."

"Even with blowing the side tunnels?" Fargo asked.

"Even with that," Hank said. "We still have a few hundred sticks at least."

"Where is it kept?" Fargo asked.

"Some is in a small shed tucked in the rocks away from the larger buildings in case something happens. About half of it's stored in a cool, dark area of the mine."

"Is that standard?" Fargo asked. "Would the Brant mine have the same layout?"

"No," Jim said. "They store most of their dynamite in a shed attached to the outside of their stable, right below the trail up to the mine."

Fargo remembered that building from last night. One hired gunhand had hidden behind it. He likely didn't know what was in it either, or he wouldn't have done that, even though bullets normally would never explode dynamite. It was just the idea of hiding behind a building full of the stuff in a gunfight that could turn a man's gut.

"So, miners, how do I blow up that building and their dynamite?"

Hank laughed. "Toss a couple sticks of dynamite with lit fuses in on top of their boxes and run like hell."

Walt laughed too. "Yup, that would do the job."

"So, I'll toss two sticks of lit dynamite into the building," Fargo said. "Mind getting me a few sticks and some bolt cutters to cut any lock they might have on it? Make the fuses long enough for me to get away, would you?"

All three looked at him like he'd lost his mind. And just maybe he had.

Fargo figured it was time for the owners of Sharon's Dream to push the advantages they did have. First off, they outnumbered the remaining men at Brant's mine by four-to-one at least. Most of the miners were not fighters like Brant's remaining men, but Fargo had a hunch that when pushed, they would make a pretty good show of themselves.

Sarah and Henry Brant and their foreman, Kip, had also had a sleepless night, and more than likely a very long day just waiting around for their help to arrive. Giving them another sleepless night and maybe reducing their numbers a little more might get them to make some hasty and bad decisions.

Fargo knew one thing for sure: Henry Brant had a huge ego and would hate to be beaten by a bunch of dirt diggers. Fargo had seen egos like Brant's before, and when pushed up against a wall, they very seldom made sound decisions. That was a trait Fargo was going to bank on.

For the second night it felt like someone had tossed a black blanket over everything as the sun went down. No sign of a moon, but the light from the stars was bright enough to move by if a person let his eyes adjust.

Fargo had already walked about forty paces down the road heading to the Brant mine. Jim had drawn him an exact map of where the two Brant guards were watching the road. They were up over a shallow ridge and on top of a second ridgeline. Behind them was the Brant compound and mine. But from the first ridge to the second ridge there was a shallow ravine that Fargo would have to go down and through. He needed those guards distracted some to give himself a better chance of moving up on them unseen.

He kept walking down the road as his eyes adjusted. On his back was his carbine and on his hip his Colt, shells in all six cylinders. He had four sticks of dynamite wrapped in a cloth and stuck down the back of his pants inside his shirt. He also had a small bolt cutter strapped securely to his leg with two belts.

Just before he could see the two guard stations over the first ridge, he ducked down and went toward the mountain on his left that separated the two mines, working up through the rocks silently, watching every step to make sure he didn't jar loose a rock and let the guards know he was there.

When he finally reached the position he wanted, he lay on his stomach and crawled forward a few feet until he could see them and the lights from the compound behind them.

There, he settled in to wait for Hank and his men to make the next move.

He didn't have long to wait. Along the high ridgeline between the two mines, he caught the glimpse of sparks as if suddenly the entire ridgeline had lit up.

Some of the Sharon's Dream men had crawled down over the ridge as far as they dared. Those men were the ones with the strongest throwing arms. Walt had actually tested a number of them, finding the few who could really throw a long distance.

Then they had tied sticks of dynamite to fist-sized rocks to give them more weight for throwing. Fargo doubted that any of the dynamite would actually reach the compound from the ridge, but it was certainly going to shower the compound with a lot of rock.

It was like lying under the night sky watching falling stars. A half dozen sticks of dynamite launched at the same time, their fairly short fuses burning as they flew through the air.

Fargo crouched, ready to move as the sticks disappeared behind the ridge. He had his eyes covered with one hand to keep the flash from momentarily blinding him. He needed to see in the dim light.

One guard on the ridge stood and said, "What the hell was—"

His words were cut off by the first explosion, followed at once by the others. Even with his hand over his eyes, Fargo could sense the bright light from the explosions.

He scrambled to his feet and headed for the guards, moving quickly and silently through the rocks as they both stood and watched the fireworks going on above the compound.

More sticks flew through the air from the ridge. More explosions rocked the ground as gunfire opened up, both from the ridgeline and from the compound firing back. From that distance, it would be only luck if someone hit something, but Fargo had figured that guns firing with the explosions would make it seem like a serious attack and give him good cover getting to the stable and the Brant dynamite.

Both guards had their rifles up and were standing side-by-side firing in the direction of the ridge. A new explosion was so close to them that they ran to the right, giving Fargo clearance to head down the hill toward the buildings.

At a run, crouched with his gun in his hand, he aimed for the stable. If any of the other guards saw him, he hoped they would think he was one of the road guards coming back into the compound to help out.

He made the small shed attached to the stable, undid the bolt cutters, and cut the lock with a quick movement.

More dynamite exploded in the rocks above the

mine, hitting everything with a shower of pebbles and stones. Some of the rocks even reached him. And those explosions were very loud down there in the compound. He couldn't imagine what the one he was about to set off would sound like.

He chose the two sticks with the longest fuses and set them just inside the door on a box of dynamite. He quickly lit them and eased the door closed. With the other two in his hand, he sprinted around the stable so that he was on the back side of the compound, away from the attack coming from the direction of Sharon's Dream.

Hank had told him he had about one minute to clear the area after he lit the long fuses. Only thirty seconds for the short fuses they had given him.

Hiding against the edge of a large rock behind the stable, he lit up the other two sticks together.

Then, as hard as he could, he threw them toward the back of the bunkhouse. If there were still men in there sleeping through all the explosions, they were going to get a very rude awakening very soon.

"Hey!" a guard shouted from the rocks above him, and stood, bringing up his rifle to aim at Fargo. He must have seen the lit dynamite flying through the air. He was about twenty paces above Fargo in the rocks. If the fool would have remained down, Fargo would have been in trouble, but he had decided to stand up to get a better angle.

Fargo shot him twice with his Colt before the man could get a shot off.

He had just cleared the hill and was over the ridgeline when the Brant dynamite exploded. Even over the ridge he could feel the impact, as if the air had suddenly become hard and smacked him on the back.

"It's Fargo," he shouted ahead to the trigger-happy miners guarding the road out.

As he neared them, about thirty men led by Jim gathered around him, all excited by the huge explosion that had lit up the night.

"You sure know how to keep people awake," Jim said, laughing.

"I don't think anyone in the county slept through that," Fargo said, smiling. Then he turned serious. "Take up your positions. No one gets out of that mine alive. Understand?"

They all nodded.

"Good," Fargo said.

He turned to Jim. "Make sure no one can get through the rocks between here and the ridge and down in that ravine. We have to hold them in there for the night, at least those that are still alive."

"What's going to happen tomorrow if we hold them in there?" one miner asked.

"I'm going to clean up the mess and then you all can go back to making yourselves rich with your mine," Fargo said, turning and heading down the road for the turnoff to Sharon's Dream.

"Now I like the sound of that," someone said.

From the direction of the Brant mine, the sounds of more dynamite echoed over the hills.

That was a sound that Fargo liked.

13

Fargo made it back to the big house at Sharon's Dream and headed up toward the ridge, eating a beef sandwich one of the cooks had handed him as he came out of the stable.

Every thirty minutes, more explosions rocked the area. They were tossing only two or three sticks at a time now, just enough to keep anyone in the Brant mine shaking and awake. Walt had figured that, at that rate, they would have enough to make it all the way through the night.

As Fargo came up to the base camp that Hank had set up on the Sharon's Dream side of the ridge, he was met with applauding miners.

Hank came out of the shadows, smiling. "Wait until you see what you did down there."

He motioned for Fargo to follow him on a path up to the ridge.

In the faint light, Fargo could see some of the miners scattered along the ridgeline with carbines, keeping behind the shelter of large rocks. Fargo lay down beside Hank on a flat rock and eased forward. Even though there was almost no chance of a stray shot from below hitting anyone, it was better to not take chances.

Only three lamps still burned down there, but the compound was clear. The sight that greeted Fargo shocked him, and he wasn't a person who was easily shocked.

The entire stable was gone, with dark shapes that

must be dead horses scattered everywhere. Fargo felt bad about the loss of good livestock, but in this case it couldn't be helped.

The bunkhouse was mostly gone. Except for a front wall, only a large pile of twisted and torn timber remained.

The big house had no windows left in the front at all. They had all been blown inward by the blast.

"Anyone come out of any of those buildings?" Fargo asked.

"Nope," Hank said. "They pulled one from the bunkhouse, but he's still lying down there in the open and I'm bettin' he's dead. No one has come out of the big house."

"So you haven't seen Kip or either of the Brants?"

"Kip came out of the big house just before the blast you set off, then went back inside. No one has seen him since."

Fargo nodded. "They're still waiting for their help to arrive. How many gunhands do you think are left down there?"

"Maybe ten at most," Hank said, "not counting Kip or the Brants. But we've only seen the six guards on duty. No one has relieved them so far."

"Okay," Fargo said, pushing himself back from the edge and standing. "Keep your men switching off and fresh. Keep pounding them, and take no chances. Check in with Jim on the main road once in a while."

Hank nodded. "Where are you going?"

"I have an errand to run in town," he said, heading down the hill toward the stable. "I'll be back in the morning to clean up the mess down there. Just make sure no one goes out of or into that compound until I get back."

He headed down the hill toward the stable and his big Ovaro. Thirty minutes later, after checking in with Jim and the men at the entrance to the Brant mine, he was stabling his horse in town.

He walked into the Wallace saloon and up to the

bar to be greeted by the smiling face of Reg. "Was that you that rattled my bottles a while back?"

Fargo returned the smile. "Just Henry Brant having a little mine accident. Is our fair boss around at this late hour?"

Reg tipped his head toward her office. "I doubt she was going to sleep much tonight."

Fargo tapped the bar as a thank-you. "That problem is going around."

He knocked lightly on Anne's door, then pushed it slowly open when she said, "Come in."

She was sitting at her desk, a pair of reading glasses on her nose. She pushed them down and said, "Yes?" without turning.

He closed the door behind him and said, "I hope all the explosions aren't keeping you up."

She spun around, beaming. "Skye!"

A moment later she was in his arms, kissing him hard and fast. Just about the time he was hoping that her kissing him would never end, it did. She held him at arm's length and said, "Now what have you been up to? That explosion knocked plaster off of some of my ceilings."

"It seems that Henry Brant had a little more dynamite in his shed than we thought he did," Fargo said, grinning.

"How did you—? Never mind, don't tell me. You can fill me in on everything when all this is over. I'm assuming it's not over yet."

"It's not," he said. "I just wanted to check on you, make sure you were all right, and get a little rest. The men of Sharon's Dream are doing a great job defending their mine. And Brant and his people don't know yet that help isn't coming, so they're not going anywhere. At least not until tomorrow morning after I tell them."

She kissed him hard, then said, "Good. Follow me. Are you hungry?"

"Nope. Just tired."

She led him quickly down the back hallway and up the back staircase to her room.

"Lock and bolt the door," she said as she went to draw the drapes and turn the lamp down even lower than it was.

As he finished with the locks, she turned him around and started undressing him, first undoing every button on his shirt, then pulling his undershirt over his head. Then she had him sit down and she worked on pulling off his boots, then his britches.

Before he knew it, he was sitting on the edge of her bed completely naked, his manhood thrusting up into the air.

She took hold of him, rubbing gently, and said, "I thought you were tired."

"For a beautiful woman who just undressed me, not *that* tired."

She laughed and stepped back, working quickly to undress herself right in front of him. This time she made no tease of anything, just went about the business of shedding her dress and undergarments, laying them on the chair by the window to hang up later.

There was something hypnotic about watching a beautiful woman undress, especially if there was the promise of a roll in the hay to follow.

When she turned from laying out her dress and started toward him, he felt his entire body tense. He took her all in, from the smooth skin on her neck to the large brown nipples to the thick patch of fine brown hair between her legs. Everything about her just fit together.

She came into his arms and kissed him hard. "Let me do the work," she whispered. "Just sit there."

She turned around and settled on his lap like he was a chair. He reached up and put his arms around her, holding her breasts gently in both hands.

"I'm supposed to do the work, remember?"

"A fella's got to have something to hang on to, doesn't he?"

She laughed and then her hand expertly guided him inside her.

She settled there for a moment; then with a loud sigh, she lifted up slightly and then settled back down again.

The sensation of her body holding him, sitting on him, was almost more than Fargo could bear. He slowly rubbed her breasts as she went up and down again.

And then again, letting him slide easily in and out of her while her juices flowed down his manhood, coating him.

He helped lift her on the next motion and then let go, letting her drop down on him a little harder.

The movement made her gasp and after that she increased the pace and he joined her, helping to lift her gently with her breasts while rubbing them, then dropping her again onto his ramrod-hard shaft.

He could tell that they were both getting closer and closer as they pounded again and again, slamming their private parts together.

He let his hands drop to her hips and slip under her buttocks as she lifted up again. He took over after that, lifting her, letting her go, lifting her, letting her go, faster and faster and faster.

And then she said, very intently, "Yes!"

She squeezed him tight as she reached her peak and a moment later he filled her, seeming to turn himself inside out into her womanhood.

They sat there together for a long moment, both of them trying to catch their breath.

Then slowly he softened and slipped out of her.

She stood and pushed him back on the bed.

He fell flat on his back, totally drained, looking up at her flushed face and beautiful body.

"Get under those covers and get some sleep, mister," she said. "I'll wake you at sunrise."

He did as she ordered, because he had learned over the years that when a naked woman tells you to do something, it's best to just do it.

*   *   *

The next thing he knew, she was nudging him gently. "Skye, it's almost dawn."

He opened one eye and looked at her. Her hair was mussed and she had a pillow mark on one side of her face, but she still looked radiant and beautiful.

"Thanks."

With a gentle peck on her cheek, he rolled out of the soft, warm bed and into the cold air of the room. He glanced out through the drapes. She was right—the sun was just starting to color the sky and he could hear a couple of roosters crowing.

"Go back to sleep. I'll be back when this is finally over."

She nodded but didn't close her eyes.

He used the pitcher and basin to wash his face and neck, then slipped on his britches and his pants before putting on his undershirt and shirt.

By the time he had his boots on, she was sitting up in bed, the sheet pulled up under her chin.

He stood and made sure his Colt was loaded completely. He turned to her. Even with the sheet covering most of her front, she was still alluring enough to make him want to take his clothes off and crawl back into that bed with her. But of course he couldn't.

"Lock the door behind me, and if you would do me a favor, stay inside the building until I give the all clear."

"That's not a problem," she said, smiling. "I have more than enough work to do. Thanks for worrying."

"You're welcome."

"Just come back to me, mister."

"I'm like a bad penny," he said.

With that, he turned and went out into the hallway. He stood there for a moment until he heard her lock and bolt the door. Then from the other side she said, "Good luck, Skye."

He smiled and turned for the stairs. Always nice when a woman understood what a man did and didn't try to stop him. He had run into very few women like that in his travels.

Cain's wife, Sharon, had been one of those special women. Fargo had been in their home over the years more times than he could count. She had always made him feel welcome and he had liked her a great deal.

Cain knew he had been lucky to find her, and he never once talked bad about her. When she died, it tore Cain apart. It was only the fact that he had a son to finish raising that kept him going. And the fact that Sharon would have been mad at him if he had given up and gone down into a bottle.

Now it was up to Fargo to avenge his friend, to make sure that Sharon's Dream would remain in good hands as Cain and Sharon would have wanted.

14

The sun was still only faintly coloring the sky as Fargo checked in with Jim at the Brant mine road.

"Keep your eyes open and your men on guard," Fargo reminded him.

"Understood," Jim said.

Fargo moved on, leading his big Ovaro down and into the stable at Sharon's Dream, making sure his horse was fed and taken care of.

Then, with his heavy carbine in his hand, he headed up toward the ridge between the two mines.

The sky had turned a faint blue, but the sun had yet to color the tops of the mountains. It wouldn't be long until full daylight was on them. Again, the coming day promised to be clear and hot. He hoped to have this over with before it got too hot.

At the top of the ridge, he met Hank and Walt.

"Better send a dozen more men to Jim on the road," Fargo said as he stepped up near the top of the ridge to their base camp.

Hank nodded and told another man to take twelve from along the ridge and get going.

"So, what's happened?" Fargo asked.

"We threw all but our last six sticks of dynamite at them," Walt said. "We figured we had better save those for an emergency."

"Good idea," Fargo said. "When did you throw the last ones?"

"Thirty minutes ago," Hank said. "We varied the

136

length between throwing them, so they wouldn't get used to a pattern."

"Again, good thinking," Fargo said. "Any movement down there?"

"Nothing," Hank said. "Guards are all still at their posts. They haven't been switched out, which tells me there's no one left to replace them."

"Do you have the spyglass?" Fargo asked.

Walt went back to a pack and pulled it out. "Not enough light for it to work at night."

Fargo slung his carbine over his shoulder, took the heavy metal spyglass, and moved to a position on a rock where he could see the compound below. In the morning light, the destruction seemed even worse than before. Except for the big ranch house, which had all of its windows blown out, there was almost nothing left down there.

He had Walt tell him where the six guards were stationed, and he checked out each one. Two of them were asleep; the other four were nodding.

Six guards at posts. No bunkhouse left to hold any others, so those that were still alive were in the big house with Brant and Sarah and Kip.

That meant there were nine survivors total, maybe a few more, but not many.

Fargo spent a few minutes with the spyglass scouting the hillside below him for a way down and a place that had good enough cover and was close enough for the Henry to do its work. All the dynamite had really changed the hill above the mine, but finally Fargo found what he was looking for.

He slipped back off the rock and handed the spyglass to Walt. "I'm going down there. If I get pinned down, I'll shout for help. But unless I do, you stay here and keep your people at their posts."

"Nothing at all we can do?" Hank asked. "This is our mine. Cain was our boss."

"I understand that," Fargo said, "but he was my *friend*."

He went on before the two good men could argue. "You've done everything you can. This is my fight now and I like to go it alone. If I need help, I'll shout out."

Fargo turned to start over the ridge, then thought better of it and turned back to the two men. "If something happens to me, I want you to carry on. You know what Brant did to Cain. Take care of the bastards for me."

Both men nodded and said nothing.

Fargo turned and headed up over the ridge, not spending too much effort to hide as he went, but moving fast and staying in what cover he could.

He made it all the way to the rock he had picked out for cover without a shot coming his way. The guards were either asleep or had lost the will to fight. It didn't much matter to him.

Fargo slid up on the rock and pulled down on the guard slightly below him, the one closest to the mine tunnel. That was the guard that had the best angle on him and the one Fargo needed to take care of sooner rather than later.

The shot seemed very loud as it echoed over the silent compound. The guard he had targeted snapped around and slumped over a rock, a moment later sliding to the ground, leaving a bloody trail on the rock.

Fargo slammed another shell into the chamber and quickly took out the guard in the rocks above the destroyed bunkhouse.

That man fired into the air as Fargo's lead ripped through him.

The other four guards opened up on Fargo as he slipped back slightly into more cover. He could take his time with those four. He had the angle and the advantage on them.

With a fresh cartridge in the chamber, he waited until they had all fired, then eased up and took out the guard closest to the road.

He hit the second guard beside the road next.

Fargo slid back as the last two guards fired on him.

From around the edge of the rock, he could see the big house. No movement from there at all.

"Fargo," one of the two guards yelled. "How about we just call this a draw and get out of here? We have no fight with you."

"Your boss won't like it."

"Haven't seen him all night," the other guard shouted. "More than likely he's dead in the house from the dynamite blast."

Fargo yelled, "Get out of here."

"Thanks," the first guard shouted back.

As Fargo watched, the two men stood and climbed out of their guard posts, heading for the road.

Fargo then eased up on the rock so he could check the compound completely. There was nothing left moving at all.

Nothing. Not even a slight wind to blow around some of the dust from the night of explosions.

"Those still in the big house," Fargo shouted into the silence. "I have some bad news. The men you hired aren't coming. The entire gang of them, including Mick Rule, is lying in the morgue in Sacramento. If you don't believe me, just ask Marshal Davis."

No movement, no sound, nothing came from the big house.

Fargo checked the compound one more time for any sign that any man was still alive, then eased out of hiding and headed down the hill toward the big building, keeping his attention focused on the black openings of the blown-out windows.

He took his time, moving from cover to cover, until he finally reached the side of the building with no windows. He stopped there, again staring at the compound, at the mine entrance, at the ruins of the buildings, waiting and watching for any movement.

On the ridge back toward Sharon's Dream, he could see a few of the miners standing on rocks, watching him. They had lost all fear of a stray shot hitting them now. They figured there was no one left to shoot at them.

Fargo put his carbine over his shoulder and took the heavy Colt from its holster. Then he eased onto the front porch, moving slowly in the splinters of wood and small stones. There was no glass, since it had all been blown inside.

From the looks of the destruction, he was starting to wonder if he had killed the Brants with the explosion.

He stepped through what had been a large window with a low sill and into the dark insides of the ranch house, freezing in place with his Colt ready to send lead.

This had been a living room, but much of the furniture was smashed against the wall or out behind the large building. He could see through the back windows that even the two-seater outhouse had been knocked over, and a couch that had been in this room lay tipped on top of it.

Two bodies were thrown against the back wall between two windows. One was impaled by a long spike of wood that had nailed him to the wall like a wild animal.

Both had been killed by the blast, their skin completely shredded by flying glass.

Neither of them was Henry or Sarah Brant or Kip.

It was starting to look more and more likely that no one in this building had escaped the explosion. There had been too many windows, and the main force of the blast had hit the big house almost directly. It was lucky the building was even standing.

Still, being careful in every room, Fargo searched the big place, moving as silently as his boots on the broken glass would let him.

He found two other bodies in the kitchen, both cooks.

He found another body, a guard, in a bedroom. He had probably been using the room and the window as a guard post.

And still no Kip, Henry Brant, or Sarah Brant.

Fargo went back through the house and motioned for Walt and Hank to come down.

As the two miners climbed down the rocky slope, Fargo checked the compound completely, making sure there were no surprises left, no men left alive.

When Walt and Hank reached Fargo, he said, "They escaped. One of you get Jim and about ten men from up the road to come down here and check that mine, make sure no one is in there. Tell them to go in with guns drawn and bring out anyone who might be in there. And tell him to leave some men guarding the road. This isn't over yet."

Walt nodded and headed at a run up the road. When he reached the second rise, he started shouting, "Jim, it's me, Walt. I'm coming up the road. Fargo wants you and some men."

Fargo nodded. Smart kid. He was taking no chances of getting shot by a tired miner with a hair trigger.

Fargo turned back toward the main house. They had last been seen in that house. That was where their trail started; that was where he would start.

He went through the house and out the back. Then he turned and looked up at the ridge, moving around until he found a place where someone could move behind the building and not be seen from the ridgeline. After a short time, he had their tracks. They went along the side of the house into some brush and rocks and then up into the canyon. Three sets of tracks led into the canyon, one of them a woman's.

Hank followed Fargo through the building, looking ashen at the sight of all the dead bodies.

"Where does that canyon lead?" Fargo asked, standing beside the tracks. "That's where they went."

"It goes nowhere. It's a box."

"No trail out?"

"Not that a horse could follow."

"They weren't on horses. Where's the closest ranch or mine from here in that direction?"

"The Toole Mine," Hank said. "Played out and abandoned about two years ago. A very rough full day's hike on foot, but they would have to get out of that canyon first."

Fargo looked around at the hills and rough terrain towering behind the mine. "Any chance they could circle around and get back to the Placerville road?"

At that moment, Jim and Walt joined them, coming through the house, their boots crunching on glass.

"No one lived through this," Jim said, stepping down to stand beside Fargo and Hank.

"Men are searching the mine," Walt said.

"Brant, his daughter, and Kip got out before the blast, headed up into the canyon," Hank said.

Walt laughed and looked at the canyon. "You're kidding."

Jim shook his head. "In the dark, I'd wager they didn't get far in those rocks."

"It's been light enough to move for an hour," Fargo said. Then he repeated his question. "Could they circle back to the Placerville road?"

"No chance of circling back," Jim said, and both Hank and Walt nodded their agreement. "The only way out of that area is the Toole Mine road. Or back this way."

"Or," Hank said, "climb out of the canyon on the left side, go around Mary's Peak there, and come down the creek into Sharon's Dream."

"So we cover all three ways," Fargo said. He turned to face the three miners. "I don't want any of them to get away."

15

Fargo figured out his plan. "Walt, get two more sticks of that dynamite and blow them on the hillside like you were doing all night. And keep it up every thirty minutes or so. I want Brant to think it's still a stand-off here."

Fargo turned to Hank. "Get some men and get the bodies cleared out of here, then set your men to guard this house and not let anyone out of that canyon, just in case someone gets past me."

"You think Brant has a hideout back up in that canyon?"

"I guess we'll find out," Fargo said.

He strode over to the Sharon's Dream side of the house and glanced at the ground, then followed the tracks to the edge of the rocks. He quickly pulled some sagebrush away that had been hiding wagon tracks leading back into the rocks.

"They couldn't leave this way because you would have seen them, so they went out over the rocks on the other side of the house. Then, more than likely, a few hundred paces up the canyon they doubled back to this trail. It would have been an easy walk in the dim light."

"Why have a hideout up there in a box canyon?" Walt asked.

"The same reason Cain always moved his gold ore out to Sacramento every time he had a full load," Hank said, starting to smile.

Fargo nodded. "To keep it safe."

"I wondered why Brant very seldom moved ore into Sacramento," Jim said, shaking his head. "He probably kept most of it up in that canyon."

"He wanted people to think his mine was playing out," Walt said. "To give him a reason for going after Sharon's Dream."

"Maybe it was playing out," Fargo said. "But going after Sharon's Dream was probably just his need to always have more. I know the type."

Fargo turned and started up the trail, his carbine off his shoulder and a shell in the chamber. "I have a hunch the owners of Sharon's Dream are going to become a little richer very soon."

Fargo moved carefully up the winding trail, staying in as much cover as he could.

About a hundred paces up, he saw where the three had come out of the rocks and turned into the box canyon.

He studied their tracks, making sure there were only three. There might be a few other guards up there, but he doubted it. The box canyon walls would give Brant a feeling of security, but still, Fargo was going to take no chances.

He waited for a few minutes until the two sticks of dynamite rocked the air. That would let anyone up in the canyon think that nothing had changed at the mine.

He left the trail and moved through the rocks, keeping low, stopping regularly to study the shadows and vantage points ahead of him in case there was a guard post set up along the road.

It took him a full hour to get within sight of the house and large stable tucked against a rock face on the right side of the box canyon. The rock walls towered far higher than the tallest trees, and most of the walls were sheer. Even on one side where there had been a rockfall, Fargo doubted anyone could climb out of here without ropes.

In the back of the canyon on the left side, the wall

was stained with the remains of a dry creek. During rain, it must be a pretty spectacular waterfall, but in the summer it was just a dry, watermarked wall with not even a drop of water in the big depression below the falls.

Even animals would have no reason to come up this canyon.

No guards were posted anywhere that Fargo could see, and there was no sign at all of Brant or Sarah or Kip.

The house surprised him because of its size. It had to be as large as most farmhouses, and was painted white and looked well kept. It was two stories, with a wide front porch and curtains in the windows. It looked like it belonged on an open range, not tucked among the rocks in a box canyon. And the stable against the rocks was also large, clearly intended to house horses and maybe a wagon.

It was no wonder Brant and Sarah and Kip had come back here. This place was as comfortable as the big house. And would allow a lot better night's sleep while they waited for their help to come.

Behind him, now mostly blocked by the walls of the canyon, the sound of two more explosions filled the air, keeping up the ploy that nothing had changed at the mine. He was finally going to get his crack at Brant.

The morning light was still a long way from reaching the canyon, making it feel earlier than it really was in the deep shadows.

Suddenly, the back door of the house opened and Henry Brant walked out, closing the door behind him as he went. He wore the same type of suit jacket and black pants that he had worn in the saloon. He had a small-brimmed hat perched on his head. He moved to the stable without even looking around, opened the door, lit a lantern, and went inside. Fargo watched as he picked up a bucket and moved toward a stall area, then came back, picked up another bucket, and closed the door.

There were horses in that stable and from the looks of it, he planned on taking care of them.

Fargo had seen one other thing through that open door that surprised him—the stable hid the entrance to another mine tunnel.

Why hide a second mine? Why build this up here?

With Brant busy in the mine building, Fargo decided to move.

He quickly made it down to the covered porch and then up to the front door, his Colt solid in his hand.

Standing with his back against a wall, he stole a glance inside the house, looking over the lace curtains that came halfway up the window. The room looked well furnished and clean. There was no one in sight.

He moved to the door and opened it quickly and silently. He stepped inside, ready to jump back to cover if he needed to.

No movement, no sounds at all.

He eased the door closed and stood quietly.

There was a fresh bread smell, and the smell of lilac perfume.

Was it possible that Sarah Brant and Kip were still asleep? In the deep canyon, the light outside still seemed like it was early in the morning. Or they could be in the kitchen, but he could hear no sounds coming from the back of the house.

A bed squeaked softly upstairs.

He eased over and silently went up the wooden stairs, keeping his feet to the outside of each step.

There were three closed doors in the dark alcove at the top of the stairs.

He leaned carefully against one door, listening. No breathing or snoring or movement from inside.

He moved to the second door and could hear heavy breathing and movement, but the sounds seemed muffled.

He moved to the third door. No sounds.

Whoever was still up here was in the second room.

With his Colt up and ready, he eased open the door.

There were not one, but two people in the room.

Sarah Brant lay naked on her back while Kip moved on top of her, pumping her slow and easy. Considering what they were doing, they were making very little noise.

Fargo figured they had done this often and knew Henry Brant's morning routine very well.

He checked out the room. This was clearly where Kip slept, and his britches and gun belt were hanging on the bedpost.

Sarah Brant's eyes were closed tight and Kip was picking up some speed. Fargo could see no point in letting them enjoy themselves and finish.

"I'd love to stay and watch," Fargo said, "but I have some business to attend to."

Both of them jerked hard and Kip rolled sideways, away from his gun belt.

Sarah tried to cover her charms.

"Does your father know about this?" Fargo asked.

"How did you get in here?" Kip demanded, trying to act tough even though he was naked and staring down the wrong end of Fargo's Colt.

"I came through the front door and walked up the stairs," Fargo said.

Kip opened his mouth, then shut it again.

"We can make a deal," Sarah said.

"Too late for a deal."

"Talk to him, Kip. He'll listen to you."

"She's right, Fargo. We can make a deal. I don't blame you for hating us. Cain was your friend. But he's gone now. No sense in you turning down a good amount of money and riding off free and clear."

In other circumstances their movements would have been amusing. Both of them were trying to cover their private parts with little success.

But then Kip made another move and it took Fargo a long second to realize what the naked man had done. He'd flung himself to the side of the bed where his holster hung. He grabbed the gun and pitched himself to the floor. His intention was to use the bed as a shield. He'd fire from behind there.

"Kip!" Sarah Brant cried.

Just as she shouted, Kip's head came up over the bed. So did his gun. He fired off two shots without realizing that Sarah had twisted around and was directly in his line of fire. One of the bullets struck her in the face, the other in the throat.

"Sarah!" Kip cried, his eyes reflecting the horror he felt at killing his lover.

But that was his last word and last thought. Fargo put a bullet into his forehead. It took only one.

A silence. And in the silence the odors of death and gun smoke. This had been a bloody mission and for all the slaughter Fargo felt strangely unsatisfied. Sometimes it seemed that the only way violence could be stopped was with more violence. And for every life he took he knew that he was changed, hardened, in ways he did not necessarily like. Or admire. Sometimes you had to wonder if you were any better than those you killed.

A footstep. A voice. "You killed my daughter, you sonofabitch."

Fargo turned slowly to see Brant standing in the doorway, a snout-ugly sawed-off shotgun in his hands. Fargo's Colt looked pretty punk by comparison.

"I'm afraid that honor went to your good friend Kip, Brant. Your daughter moved in front of him when he was trying to kill me. She took the bullets."

Tears filled the man's eyes as they focused on the sight of his daughter stretched across the mussed bed.

"She was all I had. And one way or the other, you're responsible for her being dead."

Any other human being, Fargo would have felt pity for the ashen, sorrowful man in front of him. But not this one. He'd killed Cain for no other reason than greed.

Fargo stared at the ugly twin eyes of the sawed-off. He was facing execution.

"You keep saying she's dead, Brant. You don't know that for sure and neither do I."

Brant's glistening eyes lifted to meet Fargo's. "What the hell are you talking about?"

"People don't always die when they get shot. Maybe she's still breathing. Maybe you can get her to a doctor."

"You're just saying that." But his voice and eyes changed subtly. They reflected a reluctant hope. Maybe she wasn't dead after all. Maybe the most precious thing of all to him could be saved.

"Look at her. I thought I saw her breathing but I didn't have time to check after you walked in with that sawed-off."

"You're tricking me, Fargo. And I won't put up with it. I'm not some fool."

"Well, look for yourself."

And how could the man resist? He not only let his gaze stray, he let it settle on his daughter for two seconds too long.

Fargo dove to the side of a chair while Brant, enraged, cursing, spent his only two shells on trying to track Fargo.

Fargo got him clean, twice. Once in the forehead, once in the heart. Brant shouted, teetered forward, then fell backward, dead.

Fargo came from behind the chair and looked at the dead man. There was no pleasure in the killing now. He'd rather have Cain alive. Not even avenging his death made up for the loss of him.

Soon enough, Fargo left.

16

Fargo walked slowly back down the trail to where Hank and Walt and Jim waited for him.

"It's over," he said. "Keep guards on the road, but otherwise, get some men to start cleaning up the new addition to Sharon's Dream."

The smiles on the three men could have lit up a night.

"What happened?" Walt asked.

Hank handed Fargo a canteen and he drank long and hard before he answered the young miner's question. He felt numb, the anger gone. All he really wanted to do was get on his horse and ride. But he knew Cain would want him to stay around for a short time and make sure Sharon's Dream wasn't threatened, that it and its new addition were headed in the right direction.

When he finished drinking, he said, "I'll show you. And bring a couple of extra men along and some shovels. There's a mess to clean up. And we need to figure out why there's another mine hidden up there."

"Another mine?" Jim said, his smile threatening to break out of the sides of his face.

Fargo shrugged and turned back up into the box canyon. "Let's go take a look."

He walked slowly and alone so the others could round up some other men and follow along. It felt better anyway, walking alone for the moment. It gave him time to gather himself a little. The three caught up with him about halfway up the mile-long canyon.

When they reached the big, white house tucked in

the back of the box canyon under the rock walls, all three men were stunned.

"Why build this here?" Hank said.

"I've been wondering the same thing," Fargo said.

Fargo pointed to the upstairs. "The mess is up there. Bury them together in the same grave and don't mark it. And I'd take that bed out of that one room and burn it, along with their clothes."

Hank turned to the men coming up behind them with shovels and gave the orders as Fargo headed for the stable. Inside, a lantern filled the place with light, and the smell of fresh hay greeted him like an old friend.

Two beautiful chestnut mares were in stalls. They looked well groomed and well fed. Brant had taken care of his animals, if nothing else.

To the right of the big stable, a mine opening ran back into the rocks, well supported and dark.

Henry Brant's coat was hung on a hook and Fargo picked it off and checked the pockets before giving it to Hank to toss with the rest on the fire.

"My guess is that somewhere in that house," Fargo said, "or in here, is his land deed and claim for this mine. Better we find it and other personal papers to make the transfer easier."

"Good idea," Jim said.

Walt had moved over to the opening of the mine and had taken a lamp off the hook. "This is well built and all the trailing was taken down the hill. Let's find out why." With that, Walt lit the lamp and started into the mine.

"Stop!" Fargo shouted to Walt. "Don't move a muscle."

Walt froze about ten steps inside the mine entrance like a statue in a city park. "You want to tell me why?"

"If Brant's gold is back there, if this mine was dug to hold his gold, which I'm guessing it was, he's going to have it rigged to kill anyone who shouldn't go in there."

"Shit," Walt said softly.

Fargo and Jim and Hank all grabbed and lit lamps.

With four lamps, the inside of the mine looked like it was outside on a bright, sunny day. And Fargo had been right. Two steps in front of Walt was a trip string about ankle-high off the ground.

Fargo moved up to it and pointed to the string, following it back into the wall to two shotguns dug into and hidden in the rock wall.

"Now, that is just nasty," Jim said.

"Everyone move back," Fargo said, putting his lantern on the ground just short of the string. "Hank, Walt, get bridles on those horses and get them out of here. This is going to be loud."

When they were ready, Fargo grabbed Henry Brant's coat from where Jim had tossed it over a stable railing. He wadded it up into a ball and, standing in the mine entrance, he tossed the coat at the string, then ducked back to cover his head and face from any sprayed rocks or buckshot.

The sound of the two shotgun explosions filling the mine made his ears ring.

Walt's face was white as he stared into the swirling dust of the mine. "Fargo, let me say one more time, thank you."

Fargo patted the big kid on the shoulder. A moment later a half dozen men came running into the stable to make sure they were all right.

They had to wait for the dust to settle before they dared try going into the mine again, so Fargo went out and sat on the front porch of the white house, staring at the rock cliffs around him while the men worked to dig the grave a hundred paces away and pile up the personal belongings of the Brants and Kip. The sun still hadn't reached the canyon floor and more than likely when it did, it would stick around for only a short time.

After the grave was finished, four men brought the body of Henry Brant down the stairs and tossed him in the deep, narrow hole.

152

The thud of his body hitting the bottom of the six-foot drop drained some more of the anger from Fargo. Maybe there was something to be said for attending a funeral after all.

Next they brought the body of Kip, wrapped in the rug that had been beside the bed in his room. They tossed him in facedown.

Last they brought Sarah Brant down wrapped in the bloody sheet and blankets that had been on the bed. They tossed her faceup on top of Kip. Then a couple of men dumped some lye on the bodies and started filling in the hole.

Fargo sat there, saying nothing, as the hole filled and then five or six men moved a few large, boulder-sized rocks on top of it, leaving nothing showing but some disturbed ground.

"Good enough," Fargo said, feeling satisfied that Cain was now avenged. He was going to miss his friend, but at least his killers had been given their just reward. He stood and said to the other men: "Let's go see if the mine is cleared out."

It was, and they found no more traps along the way.

In a wide area fifty paces back into the cool mountainside, wooden cases were stacked along both walls.

Jim yanked off the top of one and stared.

Walt yanked off the top of another and stared at it in the same way.

Hank counted the cases, his voice getting louder and louder as he went along.

There were two hundred and eighty-six cases of gold ore, just waiting to be taken to Sacramento to be sold and processed. More money than Fargo wanted to ever think about.

Fargo smiled. Not only had the people who worked for Cain gotten a very good deal by getting Sharon's Dream when he died, but by defending it they had also gotten very rich very quickly.

"Why would Brant do this?" Walt asked, moving from one stack to another, touching each top box.

"Some people don't trust banks; some don't trust

coin or paper money either," Fargo said. "Brant was rich as long as this was here. Now I understand why he built such a nice house up here."

"He wanted to stay comfortably close to his money," Hank said.

"Just like putting it under his mattress," Fargo said, laughing.

Two hours later, while the sun was still high overhead, Fargo climbed on his big Ovaro and headed back into town. They had found Brant's deed to the mine and his personal papers. Jim said he could copy the signature easily, so tomorrow morning they would appear in front of a judge with a paper stating that Brant was signing over all interest in his mine and all his property to the men and women who owned Sharon's Dream.

And the official story was that Fargo chased Brant and his daughter off in the middle of the night, letting them live only if they signed the paper.

No one would believe that, of course, but there would be no one to challenge it, and the bodies were so well hidden, Fargo wondered if the devil himself would run across them.

Again, he went into the Wallace through the saloon batwings. Anne Dowling looked up at him and smiled. She came around the bar and in front of a dozen men playing poker, kissed him hard and long.

When she broke it off, she got a round of applause from the men and some somewhat off-color remarks. She just smiled at the men in the room and took Fargo by the hand and led him into her office, where without a word she kissed him hard and long once again.

When she finally pushed back, he said, "Now, ma'am, I sure hope you don't greet all your customers like that. You're apt to wear out those lips."

She laughed and kissed him again. Then she said, "I can see in your eyes that it's over."

"You can?" he asked.

"Skye Fargo, I can read you like a professional

poker player reads a rube. The anger is gone. You want to tell me about it?"

"Long story," he said. "How about over a steak? It feels like I haven't eaten for a week."

"Sounds great to me," she said.

"Tonight, though, I'm buying."

With him escorting her, they went through the bar, into the hotel, and then into the dining room, where by the time the dessert was served, he had told her everything that had happened since he'd left her bed that morning.

"A mine full of boxes of gold ore?" she asked. "You're not kidding, are you?"

"Nope, not kidding. But I need a favor from you again."

"Anything," she said, squeezing his hand.

"I need you to arrange that same judge tomorrow to transfer the ownership." He told her what Jim was doing in Henry Brant's handwriting.

She laughed. "I'll set it up in the morning. I'm sure there won't be a problem. And I think everyone in town will be happy the explosions have stopped so we can all get some sleep." Then suddenly she looked serious and a little sad. "When are you heading out on the trail again?"

They both knew he would leave. Any thought of staying in one place too long made him feel like he was living in the bottom of that box canyon with walls trapping him. But this time he smiled at her question instead of ignoring it.

"Sharon's Dream has hired me to guard all their shipments to Sacramento. And after what they found in that canyon, and their normal production, I'm going to be around for a while yet."

Again her face lit up and her green eyes sparkled. "Then we have some time together?"

"We have some time," he said, smiling.

"Well, I suggest we make the most of it, then. I'll be right back."

He sat, sipping the last of his drink. He had lost

one old friend, but gotten closer to another old friend. Sometimes the balance in life was just that way.

Anne came back across the dining room toward him, smiling.

She noticed that his glass was empty and motioned for the waiter to bring him another. Then she sat down.

"What did you need to do?"

She touched his hand and smiled. "I figure that if I get another drink in you, I might be able to convince you to come back to my room and crawl in that wonderful bathtub of mine with me once again. So I had it filled."

"You expect me to take two baths in the same week?" He laughed, looking into those sparkling green eyes. "Are you trying to turn me into a gentleman or something?"

She smiled at that, then reached forward and kissed him softly, then whispered, "I just like it when you watch me bathe."

He swallowed hard, remembering the last time they had been in that tub together. "And how long will it take them to fill the tub?"

She laughed. "About one drink's worth of time."

"I can drink real fast."

LOOKING FORWARD!
**The following is the opening
section from the next novel in the exciting
Trailsman series from Signet:**

**THE TRAILSMAN #325
SEMINOLE SHOWDOWN**

*Indian Territory, 1860—
where a trail of tears leads Skye Fargo
into a showdown with deadly danger.*

"Don't move, mister, or I'll blow your damn brains out."

The big man in buckskins stood absolutely still. A touch of amusement lurked in his lake blue eyes as he asked, "What about my hands? Do you want me to put my hands up?"

"Uh . . . yeah, that'd be good, I reckon. Put your hands up."

Skye Fargo lifted his hands to shoulder level. A faint smile tugged at the corners of his wide mouth, nestled in the close-cropped dark beard. But he was wary at the same time, because even though he could tell from the voice that the person who had threatened him was undoubtedly young and probably inexperienced, a bullet fired by such a person could still take his life.

"You want to be careful with that gun, whatever it is," Fargo advised. "Don't let your finger rest on the trigger, or you're liable to shoot before you really mean to. And I don't think either of us wants that."

"You just let me worry about when I shoot. Who the hell are you, anyway?"

"A friend," Fargo answered. "I'm looking for Billy Buzzard."

That brought a sharply indrawn breath from the youngster behind him. "You're a friend of Billy's?"

"That's right. We rode together a while back, doing some scouting for the army."

"Oh, my God. You're him. You're the Trailsman."

Fargo had to grin at the tone of awe in the kid's voice. That was one of the advantages—or drawbacks, depending on how you wanted to look at it—of having a reputation.

"Some call me that," he admitted. "But my name is Skye Fargo."

"You wouldn't be lyin' to me?"

"Nope."

"Well, then, I, uh, I reckon you can put your hands down, Mr. Fargo. I'm sorry I pointed this here—"

The sudden roar of a shot drowned out whatever the boy had been about to say.

Fargo felt as much as heard the wind rip of the bullet's passage close beside his right ear. He whirled around, thinking that the boy had accidentally pulled the trigger, just as Fargo had warned him he might.

He caught a glimpse of the youngster's face, though, which looked even more surprised than Fargo expected, and the next second another shot blasted somewhere nearby. A narrow branch leaped from a tree, cut off by the bullet.

Fargo lunged at the kid, knocking him off his feet

and sending the boy's rifle flying. He rolled next to a deadfall and shoved the boy against it.

"Stay here, and keep your head down!" he ordered. A third shot sounded, knocking bark off the trunk of the fallen tree. That shot allowed Fargo to pinpoint the source of the ambush, because he saw powder smoke spurt from some brush atop a low bluff about twenty yards away.

Fargo's Henry rifle rode in a saddle sheath strapped to the magnificent black-and-white Ovaro stallion he'd left a short distance back up the gulch. Armed only with a heavy Colt revolver, Fargo knew he'd have to get closer to the bushwhacker to do any good with the handgun. He crawled along the deadfall, keeping the thick trunk between him and the rifleman on the bluff.

He had expected trouble as soon as he realized a short time earlier that someone was following him as he rode through these rugged, thickly wooded hills. Whoever was on his trail, though, made so much racket that Fargo had soon decided it couldn't be anybody too well versed in the ways of the frontier. Growing impatient with being the prey instead of the hunter, he had dismounted and started up a rocky defile on foot, in hopes of drawing his pursuer in after him.

The trick had worked, sort of. Fargo had figured to get the drop on whomever was trailing him and find out what was going on. He wasn't surprised to discover it was a kid, a boy about sixteen from the looks of him.

But then somebody else had opened fire on both of them, and now Fargo had to deal with that problem.

He reached the end of the log and took off his wide-brimmed brown hat, setting it aside for the moment. Carefully, he edged his head around the log and peered up at the bluff. No more shots had sounded, and the brush didn't move or rustle. Fargo's instincts told him that the bushwhacker was still up there, though.

The man was probably crouched in the brush with his sights lined on the deadfall, just waiting for any sign of movement. That tension would have stretched his nerves taut by now. A grim smile touched Fargo's mouth. He'd give the son of a bitch something to shoot at.

He picked up his hat and sailed it at the bluff.

Sure enough, a shot erupted from the brush. But it was aimed wildly at the flying hat, not at Fargo, who powered to his feet and sprinted toward the bluff. He triggered a couple of rounds in the direction of the bushwhacker, not worrying about hitting anything, just trying to come close enough to make the varmint duck instinctively for cover. That gave Fargo time to reach the base of the bluff.

From that angle, the rifleman couldn't draw a bead on Fargo, who holstered his Colt and started climbing. He used rocks and roots that protruded from the earth as handholds and footholds, and he needed only seconds to scale the dozen or so feet to the top of the bluff. He rolled over the edge and came to a stop on his belly, listening intently.

The shots would have scared away all the birds and small animals in the area, so when the Trailsman's keen ears picked up a faint rustling, he knew the bushwhacker had to be the one causing it. The man was trying to work his way closer to the edge of the bluff, maybe in hopes of being able to fire down at Fargo.

Too late for that. Fargo was already at the top, and he came up on one knee and drew his gun in the same motion as a roughly dressed man pushed some branches aside and stepped into view, clutching a rifle.

The man let out a surprised yelp at the sight of Fargo and jerked his weapon in the direction of the Trailsman. Fargo fired before the bushwhacker could get off a shot.

However, the man had turned enough so that

Fargo's bullet slammed into the stock of the rifle he held, shattering it and knocking the gun out of the man's hand. He shouted in pain and whipped around to plunge back into the brush before Fargo could ease back the Colt's hammer and fire again.

Fargo surged to his feet and went after the man, holstering his gun again as he did so. Branches clawed at him as he crashed through the brush. He could hear his quarry fleeing madly in front of him. The man was only a few steps ahead of Fargo when he broke out into the open again and lunged toward a horse tethered to a sapling.

The bushwhacker jerked the reins free, got a foot in the stirrup, and had started to swing up into the saddle when Fargo launched a flying tackle at him. He crashed into the bushwhacker, and both men collided with the horse's flank.

The shooting probably had the animal pretty spooked to start with. Now it let out a shrill whinny of fear and reared up on its hind legs, pawing frantically at the air with its front hooves.

One of those hooves smacked hard into Fargo's left shoulder and knocked him back a step. His left arm went numb. At the same time, with strength born of desperation, the bushwhacker swung a knobby fist that connected solidly with Fargo's jaw. For a second, skyrockets went off behind the Trailsman's eyes and blinded him.

Fargo's vision recovered in time for him to see a heavy-bladed knife slicing toward his face. He ducked under the slashing attack, lowered his head, and butted his opponent in the belly. The man's breath *whoosh*ed out of his lungs as he doubled up and went over backward.

Fargo leaped after him in an effort to pin the man to the ground, but the hombre threw a booted foot up in time to kick Fargo in the stomach with it and send him falling off to the side.

Now they were both out of breath. Fargo rolled over and came up on his knees in time to see the bushwhacker grab a flapping stirrup on the skittish horse and use it to pull himself to his feet. The man still had hold of the knife. He flung it at Fargo, forcing the Trailsman to dive to the side to avoid the spinning blade.

That gave the bushwhacker time enough to haul himself into the saddle and kick the horse's flanks. He kept kicking as the horse broke into a gallop.

Fargo pushed himself up and palmed the Colt from its holster, but as he brought the revolver up, he hesitated. He could shoot the horse, or he could shoot the bushwhacker in the back, and both of those things went against the grain for him. Grimacing, he climbed to his feet as the bushwhacker and his mount disappeared into a grove of trees.

Fargo thought the chances of the varmint doubling back for another try were pretty slim. Once the initial attempt on Fargo's life had gone sour, the rifleman seemed to want nothing more than to get away.

Or maybe the man hadn't been trying to kill him at all, Fargo thought suddenly, at least not at first.

That kid had been down there too, and the shots had come just about as close to him as they had to Fargo.

It was time for him to see if he could find out what in blazes this was all about, Fargo told himself.

First things first. He reloaded the Colt, then slipped it back into leather. Then he went back to the spot where he had shot the rifle out of the bushwhacker's hands and picked up the weapon with its shattered stock. There might be something unusual about it that would point him toward the owner, he thought.

The rifle had nothing distinctive about it, however. It was a Henry much like the one Fargo owned, but not as well cared for. And now, of course, it had a broken stock. A gunsmith could replace that, so Fargo took it with him.

He found a place where the bluff's slope was gentle

enough for him to be able to descend without having to climb down. As he walked toward the deadfall, he called, "All right, son, it's safe for you to come out now. Whoever that hombre was and whichever one of us he was after, he's gone now."

No answer came from behind the log. Fargo frowned and put his right hand on the butt of his Colt, carrying the broken rifle in his left as he approached. He looked over the rotting log.

The kid was gone.

At least there were no bloodstains on the ground to indicate that any of the shots had hit the youngster. He probably had a horse somewhere nearby, and as soon as he'd been able to tell that the fracas between Fargo and the bushwhacker had moved away from the edge of the bluff, more than likely he'd run down the gulch to find his mount and light a shuck out of there.

Clearly, though, the boy knew Billy Buzzard. His reaction when Fargo had mentioned the name had been one of familiarity. And he had recognized Fargo's name too, which in all likelihood meant that Billy had told the youngster about him. Fargo had a hunch that if he went on to Billy's place, he might meet up with that kid again.

And if he did, he intended to get some answers.

Then again, he told himself as he whistled for the Ovaro, he had a few questions for Billy Buzzard too.

The stallion trotted up the gulch toward him. Fargo had left the reins looped around the saddlehorn, preferring that the Ovaro be free to move around in case of trouble, rather than being tied up somewhere. The big black-and-white horse tossed his head angrily as he came up to Fargo, as if telling the Trailsman that he had heard the shots and didn't cotton to missing out on the action.

"Take it easy," Fargo told the stallion as he tied the broken rifle onto the back of the saddle. "Chances are there'll be more trouble, plenty for both of us."

No truer words were ever spoken, he thought, as he retrieved his hat, which the bushwhacker's hurried shot had missed, and settled it on his head. One thing Fargo's adventurous career had taught him was that trouble was never long in coming. . . .

No other series packs this much heat!

THE TRAILSMAN

**Available wherever books are sold or at
penguin.com**

"A writer in the tradition of Louis L'Amour
and Zane Grey!"
—*Huntsville Times*

National Bestselling Author
RALPH COMPTON

**Available wherever books are sold or at
penguin.com**

Charles G. West

"RARELY HAS AN AUTHOR PAINTED THE
GREAT AMERICAN WEST IN STROKES SO
BOLD, VIVID AND TRUE."
—RALPH COMPTON

TANNER'S LAW

Tanner Bland returns home from the Civil War to
find that everyone thought him dead, and that his
younger brother married Tanner's fiancée. So Tanner
heads west to join an old army buddy, Jeb Hawkins,
and hit the gold mines of Montana.

But the wagon train they join is not what they hoped
for. Because in the train with them are the four
good-for-nothing Leach brothers—and before they
hit Montana, there'll be more than enough blood
for all...

Available wherever books are sold or at
penguin.com